"Boxing is a man's sport.

"And I want real fighters," said Cooper, shaking his head. "Not a bunch of dolls playing around with boxercise."

The thump of the tray dropping abruptly on the table drew his gaze to Jamie. She had her hands on her hips and was glaring at him.

"Excuse me?" she asked. Her voice was low. Sexy. "You want to explain to me ~~what~~ ~~~~ ~~~~ or men?"

"Because people ~~~~ discipline and co~~~~~~~~~~~~~~~~~~~~~~~" Cooper said. "You~~~~~~~~~~~~~~~~~~~

Jamie's chin came ~~up and~~ she looked like an Amazonian warrior, ready to take on all comers. He flashed to a thought of what she'd be like in bed. Fiery, he'd bet.

"What makes you think I'm any less committed than other boxers? Or you? What makes you think that women can't handle being hurt? Ever think of childbirth?"

She was getting worked up, her breasts rising and falling rapidly as her temper got the better of her. Man, she was a handful, Cooper thought.

And hot. Damned hot…

Blaze™

Dear Reader,

Ever since I saw *Million Dollar Baby* I've wanted to write this book. Actually, the idea had been bubbling away in my head even before that, I think. As part of my partner's job, we were invited along to a K1 kickboxing event a few years ago. I expected to be bored, appalled, maybe even disgusted by the bloody, sweaty violence. Guess what? I loved it! The crowd was excited, the fighters gave their all and K1 fight night soon became one of my favorite nights out. Waiting between fights, my mind often meandered off. How can I use this in a book, I'd wonder. Hmm... And then I saw *Million Dollar Baby* and it all clicked for me.

The result of all that musing is in your hands. I hope you enjoy following Jamie and Cooper's journey. Jamie's a tough chick, a real hard-ass with a big monkey on her back—but Cooper is just the guy to help her deal with it.

It makes my day when I hear from readers. You can contact me via my Web site at www.sarahmayberryauthor.com.

Until next time,

Sarah Mayberry

BELOW
THE BELT
Sarah Mayberry

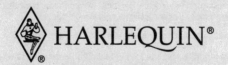

TORONTO • NEW YORK • LONDON
AMSTERDAM • PARIS • SYDNEY • HAMBURG
STOCKHOLM • ATHENS • TOKYO • MILAN • MADRID
PRAGUE • WARSAW • BUDAPEST • AUCKLAND

If you purchased this book without a cover you should be aware
that this book is stolen property. It was reported as "unsold and
destroyed" to the publisher, and neither the author nor the
publisher has received any payment for this "stripped book."

ISBN-13: 978-0-373-79408-9
ISBN-10:   0-373-79408-8

BELOW THE BELT

Copyright © 2008 by Small Cow Productions PTY Ltd.

All rights reserved. Except for use in any review, the reproduction or
utilization of this work in whole or in part in any form by any electronic,
mechanical or other means, now known or hereafter invented, including
xerography, photocopying and recording, or in any information storage
or retrieval system, is forbidden without the written permission of the
publisher, Harlequin Enterprises Limited, 225 Duncan Mill Road,
Don Mills, Ontario M3B 3K9, Canada.

This is a work of fiction. Names, characters, places and incidents are
either the product of the author's imagination or are used fictitiously,
and any resemblance to actual persons, living or dead, business
establishments, events or locales is entirely coincidental.

This edition published by arrangement with Harlequin Books S.A.

® and TM are trademarks of the publisher. Trademarks indicated with
® are registered in the United States Patent and Trademark Office, the
Canadian Trade Marks Office and in other countries.

www.eHarlequin.com

Printed in U.S.A.

ABOUT THE AUTHOR

Sarah Mayberry lives in Melbourne, Australia, with her partner, Chris, who is also a writer. When she's not writing a book, Sarah works as a scriptwriter for TV. She tried kickboxing once, but soon realized she was a writer not a fighter. When she's not avoiding exercise, Sarah loves reading, shopping, writing and going to the movies.

Books by Sarah Mayberry

HARLEQUIN BLAZE

211—CAN'T GET ENOUGH
251—CRUISE CONTROL*
278—ANYTHING FOR YOU*
314—TAKE ON ME**
320—ALL OVER YOU**
326—HOT FOR HIM**
380—BURNING UP

*It's All About Attitude
**Secret Lives of Daytime Divas

Don't miss any of our special offers. Write to us at the following address for information on our newest releases.

Harlequin Reader Service
U.S.: 3010 Walden Ave., P.O. Box 1325, Buffalo, NY 14269
Canadian: P.O. Box 609, Fort Erie, Ont. L2A 5X3

This one is for Chris. Thank you for all the laughter and love, and for teaching me so much about writing over the years. The only reason I am here is that you are beside me. I love you.

As always, big thanks to Wanda also, because she is, simply, the best.

Prologue

HE WAS A BIG MAN. Six foot three inches tall, broad shoulders, powerful arms and thighs—he dominated the boxing ring just by standing in it. Despite his size, he could move. Like Muhammad Ali, he danced around his opponents, fast and balanced, a joy to watch.

Jamie Sawyer studied his every move on her television screen, her thighs and shoulders and belly tensing, her right hand curling into a fist as he hit his opponent with a jab, then followed up with a cross to the body.

The power of the man. The elegance. The sheer beauty of watching him fight.

"He's the one," she said, sitting back in her chair. "Cooper Fitzgerald. He's the one I want."

On the screen, Cooper hit his opponent with a whistling uppercut that came out of nowhere. The other fighter's head rocked back, his eyes closed. He staggered backward. Then he hit the canvas like a two-hundred-pound slab of meat.

Reaching for the remote control, Jamie froze the image as the camera pulled in close on Cooper Fitzgerald's face.

A nose with a charming bump in it from many breaks, strong cheekbones, a square jaw, deep set navy-blue eyes, dark hair. He was a good-looking man. But she wasn't interested in his looks. She was interested in the fierce, triumphant snarl on his face and the light of victory in his eyes. He was a winner, a champion. For four years, the best heavyweight boxer in the world.

And now he was retired and starting his own fighters' gym and taking on fighters to train.

She planned to be one of them. She *was* going to be one of them. She needed him if she was going to keep her promise.

"I still like Godfrey," her grandfather said from behind her on the couch, his voice thin and reedy.

Every now and then it struck her how much he'd changed since his heart attack six months ago. The loss of his robust, deep voice was just one of many profound shifts.

"Godfrey's experienced, he's connected. He's my choice," he said.

"No, Cooper Fitzgerald is the one," Jamie said again. "He's the one who's going to put me where I need to be, Grandpa."

He knew better than to argue with her when she dug her heels in.

"Have to get him to take you on first," he said.

Jamie stood. Her legs ached from yesterday's roadwork, but she still planned on getting another ten miles under her belt today.

"He'll take me on," she said.

She just had to find the right way to ask…

1

COOPER "THE FIST" Fitzgerald adjusted the collar on his silk shirt and tweaked the cuffs on his jacket. Despite how well-made and well-cut the suit was, it felt wrong. He'd spent half his life in workout clothes, covered in sweat—he wasn't a suit kind of guy and probably never would be. But he'd come courting, and he was smart enough to know that he needed to look the part if he was going to convince Ray Marshall to leave his current trainer and join Fitzgerald Fighters' Gym.

Before hitting the doorbell and announcing his arrival, Cooper squinted at the sleek, modern house Ray had just bought. Situated on the beachfront of the increasingly exclusive Sydney suburb of Bronte, he figured the place was worth well over 1.5 million. But he already knew that Ray wasn't hard up for cash. If Cooper was going to woo him to his stable, it was going to be about more than money. It was going to be about offering him the one thing that all fighters wanted: immortality. Just like every fighter who'd ever donned leather and sweated his rounds in the ring, Ray wanted to be remembered. Ali, Sugar Ray, Tyson—no one would ever forget their names, even if Tyson was as infamous these days as he was famous. And Cooper knew he could make Ray unforgettable. He had all the raw ingredients to become a legend of the sport rather than some guy who'd gotten lucky with a few heavy purses. Together, they could fly high.

It was getting to the "together" bit that was going to take

some fancy footwork, since Ray had been with his current trainer since he started.

Aware that he was stalling, Cooper hit the bell. He was nervous. Like the suit, this was the part of setting up his own establishment that made him feel the least comfortable. He was a fighter, not some slick sales guy with a line of patter. Hell, he was only thirty-four. Not young by boxing standards, but if his body hadn't given out on him, he'd still be in the ring, giving up-and-comers like Ray a pounding. When he'd bought the gym last year, it had been with the long-term in mind. No way had he planned to be training at this age. That was supposed to come later. *Much* later.

He glanced at his hands. A scar ran across his left knuckles. He rubbed it absently. He missed fighting. Stupid to pretend otherwise. But there was no point spending the rest of his life thinking about what might have been. The doctors had given him a clear choice after he'd detached the retina in his left eye in his last fight—keep fighting and go blind, or retire.

Some choice.

"Hey, man, good to see you," Ray said as he opened the door. He gave Cooper a one-armed hug around the shoulders, the muscles of his big arms hard against Cooper's back.

A heavyweight, Ray was an inch taller than Cooper, with a broad-nosed, heavy-browed face and olive skin. He wore his dark hair shaved close to his scalp, a style that made it easier for training and disguised the fact that it was rapidly receding.

"Good to see you, too," Cooper said. Before he'd retired three months ago, he and Ray had trained together for a while. There was plenty of mutual respect between them, a good foundation for a future partnership.

"Come on in and check out my new pad," Ray said with a big grin.

Cooper followed him along a white carpeted hallway, the plush pile so deep and thick underfoot that he was almost in danger of breaking an ankle in the stuff. The hall opened into a huge living room with a high ceiling, slick black-leather-and-chrome furniture and lots of windows. The glare from the morning sun pouring through all the glass was almost unbearable and he squinted his eyes in self-defense.

"Yeah, I know, I gotta do something about that. Get some curtains or something," Ray said. "Let's check out the pool."

They passed through a state-of-the-art kitchen to a terrace that was dominated by a lap pool and a separate structure that housed a shiny gym bristling with high-end equipment, all of it visible through a wall of windows. Ray waved Cooper into one of the chairs arranged in a conversational grouping near the house.

"You want coffee?" Ray asked.

"Sure. Why not?" Cooper said.

Ray stepped toward the house and opened the sliding door a crack.

"Yo, Jimmy—coffee would be great, thanks, if the offer's still good," he called.

Cooper sat back, resting his right ankle on the knee of the opposite leg. Man, but his collar felt tight. Resisting the urge to run a finger under it like a kid at church on Sunday, he surveyed the rear of Ray's house.

"Great place, bro," he said.

"I like it," Ray said, laughing at his own understatement. He shook his head. "If you could have seen where I grew up…"

Cooper understood. The best fighters were the ones who needed it as well as wanted it. They all had their hardluck stories, some harder than others.

"So, have you thought any more about my proposal?" Cooper asked, cutting to the chase. They both knew this wasn't a social call.

Behind Ray, he caught sight of a figure moving around the kitchen making coffee. Because Ray had used the name *Jimmy,* Cooper was surprised to see it was a woman. A really hot woman, he noted as she bent to retrieve something from a lower drawer. She was wearing a uniform, a plain back dress with a zip up the front and a white apron around her waist. When she leaned over he copped an eyeful of strong, athletic legs and a tight, round butt.

Some guys preferred their women skinny like greyhounds but he'd never had a thing for bones. He liked women with breasts and butts, and strong, athletic women particularly got him going. Perhaps it was the combination of textures, hard and soft, silk and steel…

He realized Ray was talking. He'd been so preoccupied with checking out the hired help that he'd missed half of it.

"…but I've got some reservations, I'd be lying if I said any different," Ray said. "And I've got a favor to ask, if we can cut a deal."

Damn. Had Ray just said yes to him, and he'd been busy staring at some bimbo's butt?

Focus, Fitzgerald.

"I want us to be straight up if we're going to do this thing, Ray, so let me know what your concerns are and we'll deal with them," he said, keeping his gaze firmly on Ray now, even though he could still see the woman out of the corner of his eye.

"Well, you know, it's the experience thing. You've got no track record. Sorry, man, but it's true. You were one hell of a fighter, and I'd kill to have half your form, but you're freshly minted as a trainer," Ray said.

Cooper nodded. "You're right. I'm new, I'm untested— which means I'm also hungry. I like to win, Ray. You know that about me. I built a career being a winner. And I've trained with some of the best guys in the business—guys you don't have a chance of getting near because they're in the U.S. now, or they've retired. I've got a lot of knowledge and experience to pass on—and I'm hand-picking my boys because I only want to work with fighters who I know have what it takes to go all the way. You're at the top of my list, that's why I'm here," Cooper said.

"Yeah, sure, I bet you say that to everyone you're talking to," Ray said, and Cooper could tell he was only half joking.

"I'm not talking to anyone else just yet," Cooper said. "Like I said, you're at the top of my list." Maybe it was a mistake to give away so much, but he hadn't come here to shadowbox. He held Ray's eye, and the other man slowly nodded.

"Okay. Okay. I'm interested," Ray said.

Cooper grinned, and Ray grinned right back at him.

"So what's this favor you mentioned?" Cooper said, jerking his tie loose and unbuttoning the collar on his shirt. They were on the downhill run now, he could feel it.

"I've got a friend, an up-and-comer. No fight record, just starting out. Loads of natural talent, strong, fast, great power. I said I'd put in a word with you," Ray said. His gaze slid over Cooper's shoulder as he spoke, and Cooper frowned.

Was it just him, or did Ray look a little…uncomfortable?

"Fair enough. Get him to come down to the gym tomorrow. I'll take a look at him, put him through his paces. If I like what I see, I'll certainly consider him," Cooper said. That was as good as it was going to get. He had a reputation to build, and untried fighters would not do it for him.

"Uh, yeah. Thing is, it's a *she,* not a *he,*" Ray said, rubbing the back of his neck.

"Sorry, Ray, but I don't follow women's boxing," Cooper said coolly, hoping Ray would get the hint and drop the subject.

It wasn't that he thought women's boxing was wrong or freakish the way some of the old-timers did. He simply didn't think there were enough women out there truly committed to the sport. It was different for men. Often boxing was the only way out for them, and that gave them a hunger, a commitment that couldn't be faked.

"If you saw her fight, you'd know what I mean. She's good—really good. I think she could go all the way," Ray said.

"Not with me," Cooper said, shaking his head. "I'm not interested in training women. I want real fighters, not a bunch of Barbie dolls playing around with boxercise."

The door to the house slid open as the maid appeared with a tray of coffee. His gaze honed in on her instinctively, taking in her straight brunette hair, pulled high in a ponytail, the fine bones of her face, her full lips and the supple grace with which she moved. Her eyes were an unusual light gray, almost silver, and were slightly tilted. Her body was everything he'd imagined—strong and curvy, her legs long, her shoulders square and proud.

"Women's boxing is huge now," Ray said. "Purses are bigger, and the Women's International Boxing Association has really stepped things up. With women like Laila Ali out there, it's only going to get better."

"Listen, I appreciate what you're trying to do for your friend, but I'm not interested in taking on someone who's going to bail when the going gets tough. Boxing is a man's sport."

The thump of the tray dropping abruptly onto the table drew his attention back to the maid. Coffee had slopped over the sides of both cups, but she wasn't the least bit concerned. Instead, she had her hands on her hips and was glaring at him.

"Excuse me?" she asked. Her voice was low, husky.

Sexy.

"Jimmy…" Ray said, standing and dropping a hand onto her shoulder.

She shook him off, her gaze still pinned to Cooper. She was furious with him. He took in all the telltale signs—the slight flush of color in her cheeks, the tension in her body, the way she'd taken up a classic defensive stance, her weight balanced on the balls of her feet, her knees slightly flexed.

Then he got it—*she* was the wanna-be fighter Ray had been pitching to him.

"You want to explain to me why boxing is only for men?" she asked, ignoring Ray's attempts to mollify her.

"Because people get hurt. Because it takes discipline and commitment. Because it's not easy," Cooper said, holding her gaze. "You need any more?"

Her chin came up. With the sun shining on her anger-hardened face, she looked like an Amazonian warrior woman, ready to take on any and all comers. He flashed to a thought of what she'd be like in bed. Fiery, he bet, fighting for supremacy every inch of the way.

"What makes you think I'm any less committed than Ray? Or you? What makes you think that women can't handle being hurt? Ever heard of childbirth?"

She was getting worked up, her breasts rising and falling rapidly now as her temper got the better of her. Man, she was a handful. And hot. Damned hot.

"Thanks for bringing up my next point. Male fighters don't get pregnant and throw away their careers just when they're hitting their strides," Cooper said.

She gave him a scathing look, starting at his handmade Italian shoes, trailing up his silk-and-wool clad legs, up his torso until she made eye contact with him again.

"I can only imagine what kind of inadequacy a big man like you must be hiding if he can't handle the idea of a woman who can hold her own," she said.

That surprised a crack of laughter out of him. He settled into his chair a little more and crossed his arms behind his head—mostly because he suspected it would piss her off.

"Believe me, baby, this big man's not hiding any inadequacies. You're welcome to take a look, if you like," he said suggestively.

She actually took a step forward, the muscles in her jaw clenching, and Ray moved to intervene.

"Jimmy. Cool down. Go inside and take a breather. I'll talk to Cooper," he said.

"I'm not going to change my mind, Ray," Cooper said, suddenly serious. "If you coming to me is tied to taking on your friend, then we don't have a deal. I'm not interested in women fighters."

"As if I'd want you as my trainer after hearing all this bullshit," Jimmy fired the words at him. "I can't believe I thought there was a brain behind all that beautiful boxing. I guess it must be dumb luck that you can even chew gum and walk down the street at the same time."

She spun on her heel, striding toward the house without a backward glance.

Both Cooper and Ray stared after her, watching the unconscious animal grace of her movements. Once she was out of sight, Ray let his breath hiss out between his teeth and ran a hand over his head.

"That went well," he said.

Cooper waited for the other man to meet his eye. "I meant what I said. Anything else we can talk on, but Jimmy is not, and will never be, a part of our deal. Okay?"

"I hear you," Ray said. "And for the record, I'm sorry that got so…out of control. Jimmy's kind of intense. Driven, if you know what I mean."

"I thought she was your maid,"

Ray laughed, surprised. Then he shook his head. "Don't let her hear you saying that. She took time off work to come over and meet you."

"What kind of name is *Jimmy* for a girl, anyway?" Cooper asked. Not because he was really interested. He was just… curious. Which was definitely not the same thing.

"It's really Jamie, but Jimmy is a childhood nickname that stuck."

Cooper made an intuitive leap. "You're seeing her?"

Ray shook his head. "Years ago. Jimmy doesn't like to be pinned down."

Cooper got the distinct feeling that Ray wasn't too happy about that. He could see where the other man was coming from—even a few seconds in her company had been enough to tell him that Jamie wasn't the kind of woman a guy walked away from easily.

"So, am I calling my lawyer and getting him to draft a contract?" Cooper asked.

Ray's glance strayed to the house again. "I need to think about it. Can I call you tonight?"

Cooper frowned. Ray obviously felt a strong loyalty toward this Jamie woman if he was prepared to rethink a deal that had been as good as done. There wasn't anything Cooper could do about that, however—no way, no how was he taking on a woman fighter. He was building his gym, his reputation, and he wanted to win. Women's boxing wasn't going to achieve any of those goals for him, and he refused to join the ranks of has-been fighters who couldn't cut it outside of the ring.

"You know my number," he said, standing.

They were both silent as Ray led him through the house. Cooper kept an eye out for Jamie. There was an intensity to her, a focus… And, of course, there was that hot body. But there was no sign of her.

He paused on the doorstep to offer Ray his hand.

"I'll hear from you tonight," he said firmly.

"For sure," Ray said.

Walking down the path to his car, Cooper reflected that if Jamie and her fighting ambitions hadn't been inserted into the deal, he'd probably be walking away with his first fighter in his pocket right now. He swore under his breath, more and more pissed off as he thought about it.

Damn it, he needed Ray. He was young, full of promise, the perfect cornerstone for the stable Cooper wanted to build.

Some sixth sense made him glance over his shoulder before he stepped into the street. A curtain twitched in one of the front windows and someone stepped out of sight. She was probably wishing she'd slugged him one. Hell, if Ray hadn't intervened, she might even have tried.

Cooper laughed. Even though he was feeling royally pissed that her presence had soured his deal. She had balls, he'd give her that. Big, hairy ones.

JAMIE'S HANDS flexed as she watched Cooper Fitzgerald stride down the front path and into the street. He walked slowly and deliberately, head up. An advertisement for arrogance.

"Jerk-off," she said.

"What happened to 'it has to be Cooper Fitzgerald'?" Ray asked.

Jamie turned around. She shrugged casually. She'd seen so many of Cooper's fights, read so many interviews with him, she'd had one hell of a preconceived idea about what he would be like. More fool her. He might come across as witty, charming and intelligent in the media, but in the flesh the guy was just another garden-variety knuckle-dragger who saw women as living, breathing amusement parks for his genitals.

She'd known enough of them in her time, thank you very much. Hell, she'd slept with a bunch of 'em, so she definitely knew what she was talking about. Why she'd thought this guy was going to be any different from the rest of the species she had no idea.

It's because you've always been dumb about guys, a little voice whispered in her ear. It was true, too—her bad judgment where men were concerned was a matter of historical record.

"I made a mistake. I thought he was something he wasn't," Jamie said, turning away from the window. "Grandpa wanted Godfrey. I guess we'll knock on his door next."

Ray cocked his head to one side, studying her. "Maybe you ought to take this as a sign, quit before you ruin that gorgeous face of yours," he said.

Jamie made an impatient noise. "I thought you said you were going to help me."

"I did. I will. I just… I guess I don't understand why you suddenly want to get in the ring," he said.

Jamie stared at him, almost tempted to tell him about her promise, about her burning need to set things right for her grandfather, to wipe out the shame that had become her family's heritage.

"It's in my blood. What can I say?" Jamie said.

Ray didn't look as though he believed her, but he also knew her well enough not to push.

"I'll try Cooper again tonight when I call him," he said.

"Don't bother. I wouldn't take him as a trainer now if he crawled on his belly. I want someone who believes in me, not some grudging, sexist asshole."

"He's a good guy. A smart guy," Ray said.

She flicked an appraising look his way. "You're going to go with him, aren't you?"

"He's got stuff I need to know. And Lenny's getting past it," Ray confirmed.

"Good luck. You're going to need it," she muttered.

Ray smiled and shook his head, used to her lip.

"I gotta get back to work," she said. "Thanks for pitching me today. I owe you one."

"Do I get to pick what the one is?" Ray asked.

She punched one of his bulging biceps as she brushed past him, keeping things light. Ray had never really gotten over the fling they'd had five years ago. She would have driven him crazy if they'd stayed together, but he hadn't quite admitted that to himself yet. She'd done him the biggest favor of his life when she'd walked out on him. She didn't do commitment. She certainly didn't do love, whatever the hell that was apart from a really great way for a person to let herself get screwed over.

"I'll wax your car for you, but that's about as close as you're going to get to what you're thinking," she said as she headed toward the front door.

Behind her, Ray laughed. She felt the small moment of tension slide away, as she'd intended.

"Always with the mouth, Sawyer," he said.

She swiveled on her heel. "Don't call me that around anyone else, okay? As far as anyone knows, I'm Jamie Holloway, not Sawyer, and that's it."

Ray held up his hands. "Whoa, chill out, Jimmy. I'm not an idiot."

She nodded. She'd overreacted, but as soon as anyone heard her last name, they'd know. And she wanted a chance to prove herself before the shit storm descended.

Kissing Ray goodbye, she agreed to hook up with him for a training session later in the week and made her way out to her beat-up sport Ford utility. She checked the passenger-side rear tire before she got in and saw that it was running flat again. Fortunately, there was a gas station around the corner where she could pump it back up, and she'd allocated funds from this week's paycheck to cover a new tire. It was all staving off the inevitable day when the damned rust bucket fell apart, of course, but until that moment came, she'd eke every last mile out of the old girl if it killed her.

For just a second—a weak, self-pitying second—she allowed herself to wonder what it would have been like if she'd finished her naturopath training all those years ago, if her father were still alive and he hadn't done what he'd done. How different would her world look? How different would *she* look?

"Pathetic, girl," she told herself as she swung into the truck.

Twisting the key in the ignition, she waited for the engine to catch, holding her breath as she heard the familiar labored whine of the starter motor turning over. As it had more and more lately, the motor failed to catch on the first try. Closing her eyes, she banged her forehead against the steering wheel.

"Not now, you piece of crap."

She'd asked her fellow hotel maid and friend Narelle to cover for her back at the Hyatt on the Park while she met with Cooper. But if she didn't get back soon she'd be missed and the last thing she needed was another warning letter in her personnel file.

The thought of being one step closer to unemployment because she'd rearranged her life to be insulted by an ignorant ape was almost unbearable. Especially when she remembered the shiny red hunk of metal that selfsame ape had climbed out of when he'd arrived at Ray's place earlier—a Ferrari Spider convertible, no less. And here she was, unable to even get her piece of shit to start.

And he'd been wearing a suit—a dark gray single-breasted number that had clearly been custom-made for him, along, no doubt, with his white silk shirt and his fine black leather shoes. It had thrown her for a moment, seeing him dressed like a businessman. She wasn't sure what she'd been expecting—fight trunks and a sheen of sweat, perhaps? Ben-Gay and workout gear?

Whatever, it had all made him seem far less approachable than she'd imagined him to be. It had also made her feel defensive. She hated having to ask anyone for anything, but she'd psyched herself up to approach him. Then he'd walked in looking like some kind of *GQ* model instead of the fighter she'd been expecting.

No wonder he had a reputation with women. That handsome face of his, those deep set, intense eyes, that big, strong body— she defied any woman to look at him and not wonder what he'd be like naked and hard. Until he opened his mouth, that was. Then the illusion was well and truly destroyed and most right-thinking women would be either reaching for the heaviest object handy, or heading for the door.

Shaking her head, Jamie held her breath and tried the ignition again. She was about to give up and go beg Ray for a lift when the motor caught, coughing to life and belching black smoke out the exhaust.

Crowing with triumph, she patted the dash with renewed affection and slammed the truck into gear.

As always, she'd scraped through. Just as she'd scrape through being rejected by Cooper Fitzgerald. There were other trainers out there—good ones who would believe in her and see the same dream she saw. And when she was finally wearing the world champion's belt, she'd have the pleasure of cutting Cooper Fitzgerald stone cold dead.

It was an image that appealed a lot, and she was grinning fit to bust as she pulled out into traffic.

2

A MONTH LATER, Jamie forced herself to sit quietly as her grand-father taped her left hand.

"How's that?" he asked.

She flexed both hands into fists, then slid off the massage table in the women's change room and tried a few punches in the air.

"Good. Not too tight," she said.

"Let's get your gloves on," her grandfather said.

He was a little pale. Nervous for her. That made two of them. She had so much adrenaline pumping through her system right now that she was ready to jump out of her own skin.

This was her first professional fight.

"Stay warm, but don't tax yourself," her grandfather advised once her gloves were laced.

"It's going to be all right," she assured him. "I'm going to win."

He nodded and dropped a towel over her shoulders, patting her on the back. "You're a tough customer, Jimmy."

She knew it was too much to expect more from him. He'd already leaned on old fighting contacts to get her this match, despite his belief that she should wait until she had a trainer before she started competing professionally. But she was sick of being knocked back, first by Cooper Fitzgerald, then by Bob Godfrey and a string of other lesser lights. None of them had even wanted to see her fight. None of them were interested in women's boxing. She figured the quickest way to turn the situation around was to burn up the canvas with a few fast wins—then they could all come knocking on *her* door.

Bouncing from foot to foot, she tried out some combinations—jab, jab, cross, jab, cross.

"Keep your guard hand up," her grandfather instructed, referring to her left hand. "I don't want to see it away from your chin unless it's in your opponent's face."

She nodded her understanding and forced herself to be more conscious of protecting her head.

"Told you I didn't need anyone else except for you," she said, trying out some body shots now.

He made a rude noise. "I'm sixty-seven years old with a brain that's been pounded around more boxing rings than you've had hot dinners. You need better than an old slugger, Jimmy."

Before she could respond, they heard the roar of the crowd from out in the auditorium and the sound of the bell ringing.

"Okay. That's me," she said. "I'm up."

Suddenly she felt dizzy and out of breath. Careful not to show it too much, she took a handful of deep breaths.

She was going to get hurt out there today. She knew what that felt like—she'd trained in Tae Kwon Do for nearly ten years and had plenty of boxing sparring rounds more recently; she knew what it was to take a hit. But this was the first time she was going to be facing someone who wanted to mow her down, knock her out, annihilate her.

She was still trying to get her head straight when her grandfather pulled her around to face him. He held her by both gloves and looked her steadily in the eye. She stared into his watery blue gaze, forcing herself to focus, to be hard, to think of only one thing: winning.

"Okay," he said with a sharp nod after a few long seconds. "You'll do. Go take her apart."

The towel still on her shoulders, Jamie followed him out of the change room.

COOPER SAT BACK in his seat and checked the messages on his cell. Around him, the sound of the crowd filled the auditorium. It was a full house, and the atmosphere was charged with energy.

Despite himself, he could feel his heart starting to hammer against his chest. He'd probably never be able to be around boxing and not have the same visceral, instinctive reaction. He was a fighter. Even if he never stood in the ring again, he would always be a fighter, and the roar of the crowd would always lift him and fire him as it did now.

A journalist he knew walked past. Cooper shifted in his seat, made a show of checking the fight bill. He'd been fielding back pats since he arrived, and he'd just spent a solid ten minutes signing autographs. He might only be the former heavyweight champion of the world, but everyone still wanted to bask in his glow. He wondered how many months it would take before people failed to recognize him. Not long, was his guess. There would be a new contender soon, someone else the public and the media would fall in love with.

It couldn't happen soon enough for him; the mass attention wasn't a part of the sport that he'd miss very much. He'd never quite come to terms with the loss of privacy that came hand-in-hand with fame.

He saw from the fight bill that there were still another two 'exhibition' bouts to be endured before the real action began and the young fighter he was here to scout was scheduled to fight. As was becoming more and more usual, the exhibition matches were both women's bouts, part of the sport's attempts to lift the profile of women's boxing and build a following.

He considered going outside to grab a drink or make a phone call, tossing up the relative risks of being hit up for more au-tographs against the boredom of watching fights he wasn't interested in.

Then he saw her.

She made her way toward the ring with the inward-focus common to all fighters before a bout. She had a large white towel draped over her shoulders, but her long, strong legs were bare beneath the loose satin of her red-and-white trunks.

Jamie. Realizing he had no idea what her last name was, he scanned the fight bill. His finger found the names: Jamie Holloway vs. Maree Jovavich.

Jamie Holloway. Right.

He studied the old man walking in front of her. Was this her trainer? Surely not. But even from a distance he could see the old guy was a former bruiser—there was no hiding the damage years in the ring did to brow, ears and nose. Where the hell had she dug him up from?

He switched his attention back to her, leaning forward as she climbed into the ring. She flipped the towel off her shoulders. Man, she was in good shape. The ring lights caught the ripples of her belly muscles. The defined, firm muscles of her thighs glistened with oil. She wore a chest guard, but beneath the bulk of it he could discern the swell of her breasts, full and generous. Her arms were strong-looking but not too bulky—she was good poster-girl material for the boxing association, a contender who still looked like a woman. The crowd was going to love her if she could actually fight.

She wore her dark hair braided tightly back against her skull in small plaits to keep it out of the way. Her face was shiny where her trainer had greased her brow and cheekbones with Vaseline to help deflect blows. Her gaze was hard and flat as she waited.

He sat back in his chair. She'd been serious about fighting, then, that day at Ray's. He crossed his arms over his chest and wondered if her talent matched her attitude.

Her opponent, Maree Jovavich, climbed into the ring. Shorter, broader, bigger, she looked like she wasn't going anywhere fast, no matter how nicely anyone asked. He bet himself she had a hard head, too, the way she scanned the ring, marking out her territory.

He felt a stirring of interest despite himself. This might actually be a good match.

He watched Jamie Holloway as the MC announced the fighters and ran through their stats. Jovavich had ten wins under her belt to one loss. Jamie was untried, but she had two inches on the other woman in height and at twenty-seven was two years younger.

The whole time the MC went through his spiel, Jamie didn't take her eyes off her opponent, letting the other woman know she planned to wipe the floor with her. Cooper grinned, giving her full points for style. Psyching the other guy out was an important part of the game.

As the MC exited the ring, the referee called both fighters to the center of the canvas. He'd be saying the same thing referees always said, about wanting a good, clean fight, and how he was going to signal when he wanted them to break or stop fighting. Both women nodded. The referee waited for them to tap gloves and move back to their corners. Then he signaled that the round was ready to begin.

The bell echoed around the stadium. The crowd yelled as the two women zeroed in on each other like heat-seeking missiles.

Jamie wasn't shy—she took the fight straight to her opponent with a jab, followed by a left cross before dancing away from the other woman's fists. They were both good, powerful hits, and he could see Jovavich reassess Jamie as she shook off the blows and circled in again.

A flurry of punches followed, with both women landing good hits. But Cooper frowned as he began to register a worrying trend in Jamie's form as the round progressed.

The longer a fight went, the less a fighter thought and the more she fell back on instinct and habit—he knew, because he'd been there a million times. And it soon became clear that Jamie had some bad habits. For some inexplicable reason, she kept hesitating when the other woman was open, and her footwork was off. Instead of maintaining her stance and shuffling in and out, always moving, always weaving, she seemed to forget herself and lift her feet, almost as though she was going to kick the other woman or lunge toward her. The first time he saw it, he frowned. The fifth time, he swore under his breath.

"What are you doing, man?" he muttered as Jamie took hit after hit, the price for those hesitations and that poor footwork.

He could see the writing on the wall by the end of the first round, but he had to sit through all five of them and watch Jamie get pummeled around the ring before it was over. She took every hit and came back for more, even though it was clear to everyone that there was no way she was going to win unless she scored a lucky shot and knocked the other woman out.

By the time he was shaking his head in grudging admiration of her sheer pigheadedness, the final bell rang and Jovavich was declared the unanimous winner on points.

Cooper watched Jamie's old trainer tend to her in her corner, taking her mouthpiece, mopping at her face, checking her for cuts and bruises. He was saying something to her, but she was shaking her head vigorously, her gloved fists thumping down onto her thighs as she emphasized her point. Finally, the old man gave up and simply held the ropes open so she could exit the ring.

The crowd was still cheering Jovavich as Jamie made her way to the change rooms. She didn't slouch or slink away from her defeat. She held her head high, staring out into the crowd as she passed, daring them to pass judgment on her loss.

He couldn't look away, even if he'd wanted to.

Then their eyes met across the sea of people, and he saw her burning defiance and determination.

She'd be back. Even as part of him admired her chutzpah, the fighter in him regretted the lessons she was going to have to learn the hard way until she broke her bad habits—or they broke her.

Not your problem, man, he told himself. *She's nothing to you.*
He watched her all the way to the change room.

WHY DID he *have to be there*? Jamie slammed an uppercut into
the long bag two days later. She punched again, throwing all
her weight behind it.

Better yet, why did I have to notice that he was there? She
kneed the bag, then followed up with a roundhouse kick that
sent it rocking on its heavy chain.

Of all the people she could have locked gazes with in that
huge auditorium, it had to be Cooper Fitzgerald. What were the
odds? Too high for her to calculate. And yet she'd stared straight
into his deep blue eyes as she walked away from the first defeat
of her professional boxing career.

"Remind me to never let you get near me with one of those
kicks," Ray said.

He was working the speedball behind her in his lavishly
equipped home gym, the rhythmic thudding of his punches a
constant in the background.

Her years of Tae Kwon Do had given her the leg strength,
speed and accuracy to ensure that her kicks were a force to be
reckoned with. She'd been club champion for six years and state
champion for two before she'd dropped out to start training for
the boxing ring six months ago, following her grandfather's heart
attack. She thought wistfully of the days when she was at the top
of the food chain in her chosen sport, rather than the bottom. From
where she was sitting right now, they seemed a long way off.

"Let's take a break," Ray said, hitting the speedball one
last time. "You need to give yourself some recovery time
after that fight."

Jamie kept her focus on the bag, slamming another combination into it—cross, jab, cross, hook, cross, jab. She was
sweating bullets and her face ached from the bruises she'd scored
in her fight but she wasn't even close to being ready to stop.

"Not yet," she panted.

Ray shook his head.

"You are the most stubborn person I know," he said.

It was the same thing her grandfather had said to her after the fight. He'd been upset by her loss, angry that she'd ignored his advice and gone into the ring before he thought she was prepared. But she couldn't back down. She was doing this for him, to reclaim his reputation.

Since it wasn't too hot a day yet, they'd pushed the folding doors that formed one wall of the gym all the way open, and Ray sauntered straight out to where a sun lounger waited beside the pool. She watched him stretch out, momentarily toying with the idea of joining him and taking a break. But she had more work to do.

She hit the bag with another round of punches then, just for fun, some kicks. There was nothing like the buzz she got from the power of a great roundhouse kick slamming into the bag.

She wiped sweat from her brow and caught her breath. Turning, she leaned her back against the heavy long bag and opened her mouth to start giving Ray shit for having less stamina than a girl. And promptly shut it again when she registered who was standing beside the pool talking to him.

Cooper Fitzgerald.

Just like last time, she felt instantly at a disadvantage as she took in his designer denim jeans and crisp white linen shirt. His eyes were hidden behind dark sunglasses, and his hair looked as though it had been cut by one of those fancy hairstylists to the stars. He looked like a million bucks, while she was covered in sweat and bruises.

She pushed herself away from the bag and turned her back on both men. She didn't care that he was here. He didn't matter. And it didn't matter that he'd seen her lose the other night.

Concentrating on her combinations with renewed determination, she attacked the bag some more, trying to keep all of her grandfather's advice top of mind: *keep your guard hand up; shuffle forward, never step; snap your punches, don't push them; punch through your opponent, not into her.*

After four minutes of hard work, she paused again.

He was still there, she could sense him. Damn him. Why didn't he get his business with Ray over with and leave?

Sucking much-needed air into her lungs, she began to rain kicks on the bag—a snap kick from the knee, then another thundering roundhouse and a spinning back kick that sent the bag swinging.

"That's some kick you've got there."

She ignored him. *Asshole.*

"What style do you do, Tae Kwon Do? Maui Thai?"

She kneed the bag and followed up with some elbow work.

"Tae Kwon Do. State champion three years in a row, right, Jimmy?" Ray answered for her.

She spun another kick into the bag. "Two years," she corrected.

"You're good," Cooper said.

Because she was out of breath and gasping for a drink, she stopped and tugged one of her gloves off so she could grab the water bottle.

"Thanks. Coming from you, it means so much," she said.

He lifted an eyebrow at her sarcasm and, even though he was wearing those dark sunglasses, she could feel his gaze slide over her body. She felt a ridiculous, completely unwelcome surge of awareness and covered by throwing back her head and gulping water.

"How are you pulling up after your fight?" he asked.

She swallowed then brushed at the sweat beading her forehead. She knew exactly how she looked: red in the face, shiny with exertion, hair stuck to her forehead and neck. She was also sporting one badly bruised eye, a swollen lip and numerous bruises across her belly and ribs.

"I'm fine," she said. She didn't want to talk about the fight.

"You found yourself a trainer yet?"

"What is this, twenty questions?" she asked, reaching for her towel.

"Just wondering if you've got someone other than that old man to tell you where you're going wrong," he said.

Jamie's hands curled into the towel. If he had any idea who her grandfather was, he'd know how stupid he sounded right now. But telling him would open a can of worms she wasn't ready to deal with yet. She was going to face the boxing world down one day—but it would be on her terms, on her schedule.

"Don't you worry your pretty little head about me," she said. "I'll get sick of this boxing thing soon enough and go back to my needlework and cookie-baking like a good Stepford wife."

Flashing him a saccharine smile, she slung the towel around her neck and strode over to her gym bag.

She tossed her workout gloves inside and hoisted the bag onto her shoulder. Ignoring Cooper, she kissed Ray on the cheek as she passed by.

"I'll see you tomorrow," she said.

Then she headed for the house, her stride long, her head high, every muscle in her body signaling to Cooper Fitzgerald that he could go hang, thank you very much, as far as she was concerned.

COOPER SLID HIS sunglasses up onto his head, the better to watch Jamie Holloway stalk away from him.

He was still coming to terms with the way his body had reacted to seeing her again at close range. The tight black shorts and form-hugging crop top she'd been wearing left precious little to the imagination, especially when soaked in sweat from a good, hard workout. She had a sizzling body—all firm muscle, with high, full breasts. His body had gone to red alert the moment he'd recognized her, then she'd turned around and a visceral stab of emotion had ripped through him when he'd registered her bruised and battered face. He was still trying to work out exactly what that emotion had been. Protectiveness? Anger? Frustration?

As her rounded, muscular butt disappeared into the house, he turned to Ray, a frown on his face.

"Who *is* the old guy, anyway?" he asked.

"Her grandfather. He did a bit of fighting in his time," Ray explained vaguely.

Cooper swore. "You're kidding me? She's got her *grandfather* giving her advice in the ring? No wonder Jovavich ate her for breakfast."

"She wants it. She'll learn. Losing that fight is burning her up. It won't happen a second time," Ray said.

Cooper gave the other man a frustrated look. "I saw the fight, okay? She's a long way off being ready to go pro. She's got bad habits—and now I can see why. She's used to fighting with her feet as well as her fists."

"I had to be in Melbourne and I couldn't make the fight. What happened?"

Cooper slid his sunglasses back onto his face. "She wasn't ready. Someone ought to tell her that."

Ray spread his hands wide. "You think I want her in that ring in the first place? I felt freakin' sick when I saw her face this morning."

You and me both.

"Yeah, well," Cooper said, suddenly aware that he was wasting way too much time on a dead-end subject that had nothing to do with him. "I wanted to talk to you about your training schedule for next week."

He sat beside Ray as he began to outline the new training regime he'd come up with, a plan designed to build stamina and capitalize on Ray's speed in the ring. They talked for half an hour or so before Cooper checked his watch.

"I've got to be someplace else, but I'll see you at the gym tomorrow, yeah?" he asked as he stood.

"Yeah." Ray ran a hand over the bristle on his scalp, his gaze fixed on the horizon for a beat as he thought something through. "She's got another fight in two weeks time, you know," he said.

Cooper palmed his car keys. "Then she'll lose again. Someone needs to tell her to quit while she's ahead."

"She's not a quitter," Ray said, looking at Cooper as though he was the one who could do something about the situation.

"She's not my problem," Cooper said very firmly.

He was almost sure he meant it, too.

YET TWO WEEKS LATER, Cooper was watching as Jamie Holloway made her way to the ring for her second pro fight, the old man following in her wake with bucket and water and stool.

Why am I here?

He'd asked himself the same question about a million times. There was no promising young fighter to scout here tonight— there was only Jamie and her pigheaded determination. And still he was sitting here, on the edge of his seat, hoping to see a different outcome for her this time.

Stupid. Pointless. Frustrating. Because if she fought the way she did last time—and the odds were she would—she was going to lose.

He leaned his elbows on his thighs as the MC read out the fighters' stats. Jamie's opponent this time around was a girl from Queensland, taller than Jamie, more experienced. Not that that was hard.

He could see Jamie's grandfather talking steadily near her ear as she waited in her corner for the referee to call her forward for instructions. What was the old man saying? And did it matter, when she had years of training, fighting and thinking in another discipline holding her back? As soon as the pressure was on, Jamie was going to want to use her knees and legs again. And that split second of hesitation where her brain overrode her instinct was going to leave her wide open to attack. Just like last time.

Nodding one final time, Jamie moved away from her grandfather toward the center of the ring where the ref was waiting. Cooper watched the old man climb down from the ring, his movements slow.

Talk about the blind leading the blind. What a ridiculous bloody situation.

Cooper stood. He'd seen enough. Then the bell rang, and the two women came out fighting. As before, Jamie threw the first punch, a nice straight armed jab that rocked the other fighter's head back on her shoulders.

He sat down.

It didn't take long for Jamie's old habits to undermine her natural talent. And she was talented—Ray hadn't lied when he said that. She was strong, fast, quick on her feet. She had good power in her punches, good control. She wasn't afraid to go in hard and risk her opponent finding an opening. But that hesitation and that fumbling footwork let her down every time.

As the round ended and the bell rang, he watched with frustration as she sank onto the stool in her corner. She had a lot of potential. But she was never going to reach it if someone didn't take her in hand.

After the regulation minute, the bell rang and the second round started. Again Jamie landed some good punches first up, and Cooper looked to the judges, urging them to score her high. But as the round ticked into the second then the third minute, those hesitations of hers began to tell again.

"Think with your fists, not your feet," he found himself yelling in frustration at the ring. His voice was one of many, drowned out by the crowd, and he sprang to his feet, unable to watch anymore.

She was taking a pounding, her head bobbing on her neck, her steps slowing as her body reacted to the pain. He couldn't stand by and watch her go down. It was like watching a bully kick a dog.

He excused his way past the other fans to get to the aisle. Descending the stairs, he headed for the nearest exit. At least, that was where he thought he was going. The bell sounded the end of the second round and somehow he found himself smooth-talking his way past the security guy guarding the ring and barreling up to Jamie's corner where she was sitting on her stool, breathing heavily and washing her mouth out while her grandfather rinsed her mouth piece over the bucket.

"Stop lifting your goddamned feet," he barked at her as soon as he was within earshot. The ring was four feet off the ground, putting him well below her, but her head snapped around when she heard him. "You keep wanting to use your feet and it's killing your technique."

She looked dazed, a little punch drunk he figured, but then her eyes cleared and she frowned.

"What the hell are you doing here?" she demanded.

"Listen to me. She drops her guard every time she hits you with a cross. Watch her, you'll see it. Block her with your forearm, and move in with a hook. You get her right, you can lay her out," he said.

He shot a glance toward the center of the ring. He could see the ref gearing up to begin the third round.

"Why?" Jamie demanded, staring at him intently.

"Why what?" he asked, gaze darting to the ref again. Their time was nearly up; had she taken in a word he said?

"Why are you giving me advice?"

He shook his head. "I have no idea. Call it charity."

She shook her head in turn. "Not good enough. I don't take charity."

The ref gestured for Jamie to move away from the corner, but she stood there, holding his eye.

He swore. Loudly. Was he insane? Was he really going to allow some misplaced sense of guilt and sexual interest and

God knows what to push him into this decision? He had his training ambitions to think of, his reputation, his future…

"All right. I'll take you on. Now get out there and lay her out," he said.

She gave him a fierce, almost feral grin before giving her attention over to the fight.

Still not quite believing what he'd done, Cooper stood back and watched as Jamie took it up to her opponent again.

Man, but she was full of pluck.

"Name's Arthur," a voice yelled near his ear, and he tore his gaze from Jamie—his fighter—to see her grandfather standing there, gnarled hand extended.

"Cooper," he said, shaking hands.

The old man bobbed his head and Cooper switched his attention back to the fight just in time to see Jamie step inside the other woman's guard and send a smoking right hook toward her opponent's jaw.

He knew before it landed that the fight was over. The other woman's head snapped to the side. Her eyes rolled white, and she staggered into the ropes then down onto the canvas. The ref stepped in to deliver the eight count. Like a pro, Jamie kept her eyes glued to her fallen opponent until the ref signaled the fight was over.

Then Jamie lifted her arm in a single, triumphant punch to the sky.

Her first win. Despite his misgivings, he felt the rush, too. And when she glanced across at him, grinning, he grinned back.

Her grandfather was whooping with joy, and Jamie slid between the ropes and out of the ring to hug him.

"I told you," she kept saying. "I told you I could do it."

When they finally broke, she looked toward Cooper almost shyly.

"She dropped her guard just like you said, so I did what you told me to do," she said.

"I know. I saw."

She bumped her gloves together. He could feel her uncertainty. He guessed that she hadn't thought beyond this moment, she'd been so focused on scoring her first win.

"So, what now?" she asked.

"Now the hard work really begins," he said.

3

SHE HAD A TRAINER. And not just any trainer—she had Cooper Fitzgerald. Lying on the ratty couch in the apartment she shared with her grandfather later that night, Jamie lifted the bag of frozen peas from her cheekbone so she could see her grandfather where he was puttering around in the kitchen.

"He wants to see me at his gym first thing tomorrow," she said.

"I heard. Not deaf yet," her grandfather said. She could hear the smile in his voice.

She fell silent again, reliving in her mind the moment when her fist connected with her opponent's jaw and she'd won the fight. All because Cooper showed her the way. Excitement and anticipation bubbled up inside her. With him at her side, she was going to make her mark.

"He's good," she said, dropping the bag of peas again. "The way he spotted her weakness like that."

"Yep. He knows what he's doing."

Crossing over from the kitchen, he slid a plate onto the battered coffee table in front of her. Toasted cheese and ham, his specialty.

"Should have more protein after a big fight, but you know my cooking's not up to much." He shrugged as he sank into his favorite armchair and rested his plate on his knees.

He was wearing an ancient green shirt her grandmother had bought him back when they were first married, and what was left of his gray hair sat up in tufts over his ears. His once-strong shoulders curled forward with age and tiredness, and the hands that held his plate were thick and twisted with arthritis.

A fierce rush of love filled her. She adored this old man with everything she had. He'd never let her down, never betrayed her, never stopped protecting her. And now it was her turn to do the same for him.

Her critical gaze scanned the room, noting the grayed curtains, the stained walls, the chipped tiles in the kitchenette and the way the stuffing was exploding out of one corner of the couch where the upholstery had given way after years of wear and tear. Arthur Harrison Sawyer deserved better than this. In his day, he had been a boxer of renown, one of the greats who had forged a name for Australian boxers around the world. He'd fought both Muhammad Ali and Frazier before he'd dropped down a weight class and carved out his own niche. He'd fought hard and long and with enormous heart.

He deserved better.

She was going to make things better for him, for both of them. They were going to get out of this apartment. She was going to make sure he had heating in winter and cooling in summer, and that he never had to think twice about buying his monthly copy of *The Ring,* his favorite boxing magazine, because it was a luxury they couldn't really afford.

She was going to make it possible for him to hold his head high again after what her father had done. She was going to right the wrong, remind the boxing world that the name Sawyer was an honorable one, a great one, not a symbol of weakness and greed and failure.

"We'll be able to leave this place soon," Jamie said as she reached for her toast. She bit into it without testing it for temperature and hissed with pain as she burned the roof of her mouth.

"Every time," her grandfather said, shaking his head and huffing out a laugh as she lunged for her water glass.

"What can I say? I'm a creature of habit," she said with a grin.

Leaving her toast to cool some more, she lay back on the couch, repositioned her bag of peas and closed her eyes.

Tomorrow she had her first session with Cooper Fitzgerald. Things were finally on the move.

She frowned as the one reservation she had about her new trainer circled to fill her thoughts, as it had on and off ever since the fight and Cooper's unexpected appearance in her corner: she didn't know what had changed his mind about her.

She wanted to think it was because he saw the potential for greatness in her, but she was also uneasily aware that every time they'd met, he'd looked at her the way a man looks at a woman he wants to get busy with.

And she hadn't exactly not noticed the fact that he was a whole lot of man, either.

Was it going to be a problem? She opened her eyes and stared at the water stain on the ceiling.

She'd make sure it wasn't a problem, one way or another. This was her shot, and it was way more important than sexual curiosity or whatever it was that existed between them.

Sitting up again, she tested her toast with a finger before taking another bite.

"Smart girl," her grandfather said with a half smile.

"Absolutely," she said.

THE MOMENT Jamie Holloway walked in the door of his gym in the inner-west Sydney suburb of Newtown the next morning, Cooper realized he'd bought himself a whole world of trouble when he signed her on.

For starters, every single male in the gym stopped what he was doing the moment he noticed her long legs clad in tight black Lycra, her bodacious ass and her generous breasts. It didn't matter that she was wearing a loose white T-shirt over her leggings. Or that she was sporting a bruised cheekbone, didn't have a scrap of makeup on and her hair was pulled back into a tight, high ponytail. She was sexy, hot, gorgeous, and every man in the place knew it and wanted to do something about it.

And that wasn't even the most disturbing part of it all. No, that honor belonged to the fierce, fundamental surge of jealousy and territorialism he felt when all those male eyes checked her out.

Mine, his body and his animal instincts screamed. *Get your freakin' eyes and minds off her.*

He was about to embark on an intimate, intense relationship with her that was supposed to be based on mutual trust. He was about to become her *mentor,* for Pete's sake. And all he could think about was how it would feel to have her body against his, skin to skin, and how wet and tight and hot she'd feel as he slid inside her….

Shit.

Take a cold shower and get over it, Fitzgerald.

It wasn't as if he was hard up for booty action. Hell, he could pick up his phone and have a woman just as sexy and hot in his bed within the hour.

The thought didn't provide the release valve he needed and he was frowning by the time she'd crossed the gym floor and stopped in front of him, her expression open and sunny.

"You're late," he said. "Lesson number one, I expect my fighters to be punctual."

The smile froze on her lips.

"We couldn't find a parking spot. My grandfather's still looking," she said.

He eyed her coolly. "Warm up, then we'll talk," he said.

She frowned, opened her mouth, then shut it again without saying a word. Slinging her bag to one side near the wall, she pulled out a skipping rope and began to jump.

He went over to the counter near the front door and started checking some paperwork his lawyer had sent through, keeping a discreet eye on her all the while.

Slowly, the guys around him stopped gawking and started working out again.

Pathetic. Men really did think with their dicks—and he was as bad as the rest of them.

Arthur Holloway entered a few minutes later, stopping alongside the counter to greet Cooper.

"Hiya," he said, his gaze sharp as he checked out first Cooper then the gym. "Nice place you got here."

Cooper glanced around at the raw brick walls, the exposed ceiling beams, the scarred wooden floors and the single regulation boxing ring that occupied the very center of the space. A long time ago the building had originally been a grain store, but it had been a gym for many years now and the smell of leather and sweat had soaked into the mortar. When he'd bought the place he'd repainted, fixed broken windows, installed new bathrooms and equipment and updated the offices, but the place retained its old-school feel.

That and the fact that he was around the place a lot more now that he was retired had helped build membership numbers and business was booming. It didn't hurt to have pros like Ray training here. Guys who sat behind desks for a living liked to sweat alongside real fighters. Made them feel as if they were playing with the big boys.

"Thanks. You always come to Jamie's training sessions?" Cooper asked. He hoped he wasn't going to have problems with the old guy countermanding orders or sticking his oar in.

"Nope. Just wanted to check this place out, make sure it's everything Jimmy seems to think it is," Arthur said.

By which the old guy meant check Cooper out.

Cooper was about to respond when he registered that Jamie had moved onto the long bag and was pounding it with a series of powerful kicks.

"Excuse me," he said. He strode across the floorboards and didn't stop until he was standing in front of her.

She stopped. Her eyebrows rose toward her hairline as she registered his annoyance.

"What now?"

"From now on, I don't ever want to see you using your legs to fight again. You got that?" he said. "You're a boxer. Boxers fight with their fists, not their feet."

"What?" Her silver eyes flashed defiance. "It's a good workout, a good warm-up."

"You lost that first fight and you nearly lost last night because you're used to relying on your legs too much. Every time you want to fire off a roundhouse or a back kick, you lose precious seconds reminding yourself that you're in a boxing ring and only your fists are legal," he said.

She shook her head. "No way. I lost that fight because she was faster than me."

Why was he surprised that she was disagreeing with him at the very first hurdle? Had he honestly expected anything less from a woman with so much attitude?

He was tempted to yell at her the way his first trainer used to yell at him back when he was young and hot-tempered and lacking in discipline. But Jamie was a smart fighter. She learned quickly when she wanted to—she'd shown him that in spades last night when she took his advice and knocked her opponent out. He wanted to harness those smarts straight off the bat. Going head-to-head with her wasn't going to achieve that.

"You warm enough to go a few rounds?" he asked.

She looked surprised that he wasn't pressing the issue.

"Sure."

Cooper scanned the gym, honing in on Mick. At around a hundred and sixty pounds, Mick was a middleweight like Jamie and only had an inch on her in height.

"Mickey, suit up. I want you to go a few rounds with Jamie," Cooper called out.

Mick looked as though all his Christmases had come at

once. Cooper rolled his eyes. The sooner the rest of the team started to see Jamie as one of the boys, the better.

One of the gym assistants helped Jamie tape and glove up and fitted her with a padded head-guard while Cooper did the same with Mick.

"I don't want you to go easy on her," he instructed as he worked.

Mick kept throwing glances Jamie's way, especially when she pulled off her T-shirt to reveal a tight-fitting sports crop top. Cooper grabbed the other man's chin and brought his gaze back to meet his own.

"Listen to me. I want you to press her—not too hard, she's probably still feeling last night's fight. But I want you to make her sweat, okay?"

Mick nodded. Checking the laces on Mick's gloves, Cooper gave him the all clear and held the ropes for him to climb into the ring. Then he signaled for Jason, one of his gym assistants.

"Yeah, boss?" Jason asked, his attention glued to Jamie.

"Grab the video camera. I want you to get everything she does," he instructed.

It was a common enough tool—football players used tape all the time to review plays and understand their own strengths and weaknesses. Jamie was so stubborn and strong-willed that he knew the only way she'd understand his no-kick rule would be if she saw her faulty footwork herself.

Cooper glanced across to see Arthur had joined him, arms crossed over his chest.

"This'll be interesting."

"At the very least," Cooper said.

They grinned at each other. Arthur had a tooth missing, a common hazard for boxers despite the protection of mouth guards. Curious, Cooper studied the other marks that boxing had left on the old guy's face.

"You used to fight, Ray said?" Cooper asked.

"Did he? Yeah, I've seen a few rounds," Arthur said with a

shrug. He kept his focus on the two fighters warming up in the ring and didn't offer up anything more.

Taciturn old bugger.

Cooper switched his attention back to the ring.

"Okay, let's get into it," he ordered.

Jamie and Mick met in the center and tapped gloves before falling into orthodox stances and starting to circle one another. True to form, Jamie was the first to move in, feinting with her right before hitting Mick's torso with a left cross. Mick let her get a few shots in before he began to work her over. None of the hits were hard or intended to hurt, but both fighters had worked up a sweat within minutes and it didn't take long for Jamie's footwork to become compromised as she began to feel the pressure.

Cooper let them fight for a few more minutes before calling a halt.

"Thanks, Mick. Nice work. Jamie, my office," he said.

Grabbing the video camera from Jason, he led the way to his domain.

By the time Jamie followed a minute later, towel in hand and without her gloves and head gear, he had the camera hooked up to the TV and the tape ready to play.

Jamie's expression was wary as he gestured her toward a chair opposite his own.

"Make yourself comfortable," he said.

"You didn't tell me you were going to film us," she said.

"Didn't I?"

She was still breathing heavily. In the enclosed space of his office he was very aware of her scent—something fresh and bright that he guessed was her deodorant.

Instead of taking a chair, she leaned against his desk, her butt propped on the edge. He had to force his gaze away from her long legs as she crossed her ankles and leaned back on her arms.

For a fleeting second, he allowed himself to wonder what

those thighs would feel like clenched around him as he pounded into her.

"Well, go on," she said.

He hit the play button and they both watched the opening few skirmishes. As Mick picked up the pace, the first of Jamie's hesitations appeared.

"Kick," Cooper said, just in case she hadn't seen it. "And another one, and another one. You don't actually throw them, of course, but they're there. You want to fight with your feet so bad it hurts."

Her mouth and face grew tight as she watched herself make the same mistake over and over. Finally she called a halt.

"Okay. I get it. You've made your point."

He switched the television off.

"You've got some bad habits we need to break."

She nodded. "Yep. How?"

"I've got a few ideas."

He outlined them to her as she patted the sweat off her face and chest. He followed her movements with his eyes, imagining what her breasts would look like naked, how heavy and smooth they'd feel in his hands. A bead of sweat raced down her belly and he barely resisted the urge to lean forward and trace its path with his tongue. She'd taste sweet and salty at the same time, he bet....

Registering that he had a hard-on, he rolled his chair closer to the desk. He had to stop thinking like this.

"It's not going to be easy," he concluded. "It's going to take time and effort."

"I've got time. I've got effort," she said, straightening from her slouching position against his desk.

Once again, he struggled to keep his gaze on her face.

"Okay. Let's get started," he said.

She opened the door and hovered, waiting for him to join her.

"I've got to make a quick phone call," he lied. "You start in on the speedball."

She exited and he ran a hand through his hair.

His possessiveness where she was concerned, his hyper-awareness of her physically, his constant slide into sexual fantasy, the huge freakin' boner in his pants—it all had to stop. She had come to him for one purpose. She was his fighter now, not an object of lust.

He was her trainer, her mentor, her guide, and she was officially off-limits.

Man, but this was going to be one hell of a test of his willpower.

By the time she was heading into the change rooms after her first session with Cooper, Jamie knew that he was a far better trainer than she'd ever imagined. She also knew that he was the most sexually desirable man she'd ever known.

It was his attitude, the feeling she got when she was around him, as much as his body—although that was pretty damned impressive all on its own. Even though she'd taken pains to disguise her interest, she'd been unable to stop herself from watching him as he moved around the gym in between giving her instructions. His arms alone were enough to make her knees weak—solid, round with muscle, strong. When he demonstrated a technique on the speedball to one of the younger fighters, she'd paused in her own workout to watch the muscles of his back and arms in action. Nice. Very nice.

Then there was his butt. Simply watching it flex as he walked made her fingers curl. She knew from watching his fights that he had a broad chest with well-defined pecs and abdominal muscles, and she closed her eyes as she stood beneath the shower, imagining how it would feel to have her breasts pressed up against all that masculine hardness. As the water pounded down on her, she slid her hands over her soapy breasts and down between her thighs, imagining it was his fingers finding her damp and ready for him.

Abruptly she became aware of what she was doing—eroticizing her hard-won trainer on day one. She switched the water to full cold.

She knew herself well enough to understand that the simmering desire she was feeling wasn't going to evaporate. She either had to learn to control it and ignore it, or she had to neutralize it.

As she dressed, her thoughts flew to the handful of men she could call on for casual sex if and when she wanted it. She'd never been sentimental about sleeping with the opposite sex—not for a long time, anyway—and it was a mindset that had always served her well. Human beings had needs—food, shelter, sex. Not necessarily in that order, depending on what else was going on in a person's life. Right now, for whatever reason, she needed sex. Since she couldn't get it from Cooper, for a variety of very sensible and rational reasons, she would look elsewhere.

She grabbed her phone from her workout bag and called Dean, her most recent lover. He was flatteringly pleased to hear from her, but couldn't hook up until Thursday night.

Today was Monday. She frowned. She felt distinctly edgy at the prospect of having to wait that long until she could feel a man's naked body pressed against her own.

"Are you still there, Jimmy?" Dean asked when the silence between them had stretched too long.

"Sure, I'm here. And Thursday is fine," she assured him quickly. Honestly, how hard up was she, anyway? "I'll come to your place, okay?"

The one down side to living with her grandfather was that it made entertaining at her place next to impossible. Not that she was keen to inflict her dumpy little dive on any of her lovers. When she remembered the way things used to be, the beautiful things her mother had collected, the sumptuous furniture her father had insisted on...

She zipped her bag shut with a firm hand. The world had

moved on, and she was in the process of clawing back some of what had been lost. There was no point in dwelling on the past.

Steeling herself for one last encounter with Cooper before she could escape for the day, Jamie headed into the gym.

She could feel a bunch of male eyes tracking her as she made her way to Cooper's office to say goodbye. They'd get used to her. Most fighters' gyms were light on for women, but they would get over the fact that she looked different from them soon enough. Especially when they realized she wasn't about to sleep with any of them—including Cooper.

Cooper's office was empty when she ducked her head in. She scanned the gym, wondering if she'd missed him in a corner somewhere. She hadn't. He'd gone. Without saying goodbye.

He's your trainer. Like it matters if you say hello or goodbye or up your nose with a rubber hose to him. The only thing that matters is that he knows how to help you become the best.

She shook off the moment of stupidity. Her grandfather was waiting for her near the door and she forced a smile and gave him a wave.

Roll on Thursday.

She had a feeling she was going to need every inch of Dean's work-hardened body by the time their date rolled around.

HOW COULD A PERSON feel so much frustration and so much satisfaction at the same time?

It was a question that dogged Cooper over the next few days as he guided Jamie's training sessions. She was a fast learner—much smarter and more intuitive than Ray or the other two promising young guys he'd taken on. Not that he would ever voice that thought aloud—there was enough male-female politics clogging up the airwaves in the gym without him throwing another element into the mix.

She knew her body extremely well and only had to listen once when he explained something before she was able to adapt her stance or her action and demonstrate what he was looking for. She was also responding well to his retraining exercises, although she'd grumbled the first time he'd strapped the five-pound soft weights around her ankles. But the added weight at her feet was having the desired affect—every time she lifted her foot following the instinct to kick in defense or attack, she registered the extra load and became conscious of what she was doing. He was confident they would soon rid her of her that fatal hesitation—and once that was gone he had the feeling he was going to have a truly exceptional fighter on his hands.

That was where the satisfaction part came from. He'd made the right decision in taking her on. She was so driven and committed and full of potential that she deserved a chance to go as far as she could.

His simultaneous frustration stemmed from the fact that while every day brought progress in her skill level, it also inevitably brought a new form of torture for his already tightly leashed libido.

He was going insane with wanting her and not being able to have her. He'd never been so hot for a woman before. Perhaps it was because he couldn't have her. Or perhaps it was something unique to Jamie. Whatever, it was driving him around the bend and leaving him in severe danger of suffering the first case of blue balls he'd had since his teen years.

He'd had his hands on her enough now, shifting her body into position, guiding her, to know exactly how good she felt. Pretty damn good, was the answer.

But his lust had moved on from simply wanting to know her physically.

Now his fantasies involved wanting to hear that husky voice of hers cry out in ecstasy. He wanted to look into her beautiful eyes and see her lose her mind a little. She was always so focused and intent—he wanted her soft and pliant and wanting in his arms, in his bed.

So, yeah, he was just a little frustrated. With himself, with his body, with the fact that he was in an impossible situation that didn't look as if it would resolve itself anytime soon.

It wasn't as though he hadn't tried to take care of business with someone more suitable. He'd taken one of his casual girlfriends out on Tuesday night and hadn't been able to muster even a fraction of the desire he felt for Jamie. Kara was a flight attendant, gorgeous and blond, a woman he'd had plenty of no-strings good times with in the past. He'd been sure she'd do the trick, but after a bout of lackluster kissing and fumbling in his Ferrari, he'd been forced to give up the attempt as a bad joke and drive her home, shaken to realize that wanting Jamie had killed him below the waist where other women were concerned.

Really freakin' great. Talk about being between a rock and a hard-on.

Today, Thursday, he almost groaned out loud when Jamie arrived for her evening workout wearing a pair of Lycra hot pants and a teeny-tiny gym top.

Did she know? Was she doing it on purpose?

Admittedly, it was pushing one hundred degrees outside, but was it really necessary for her to flaunt what he absolutely could not have right in his face like this?

Apparently, the answer was yes.

"It's hot out there," she said as she dumped her bag against the wall. "Days like this I wish I had air-conditioning. Grandpa never gets a good night's sleep when it's too hot."

He tore his focus from the sheen of perspiration that had formed in her cleavage.

"Yeah, it's a killer," he said.

"I can work a little later tonight," she said. "I had the morning shift at the hotel, and I'm meeting a friend around nine or so, so if there's anything extra you want me to do…?"

He admired her work ethic, he really did. If he could get his mind out of her underwear, he'd probably think of something really productive for her to do.

"I want you to work on upper body strength today," he said. He indicated the weight equipment in the corner. "Let's see if we can't get a little more power into those punches."

"I'm all about the power," she said.

He followed her as she crossed to the four-station apparatus. His attention was glued to her butt the whole way. Realizing what he was doing, he snapped his gaze away and checked to make sure no one had noticed.

Nope. They were all too busy staring at Jamie's butt.

Grabbing the wide bar of the lateral pulldown machine, she adjusted the weight stack and began to do reps. He watched her technique for a few minutes, telling himself that he was doing his job and not checking out her breasts.

In desperation, he sat opposite her and started to do some tricep pushdowns. Maybe if he got a really good muscle burn going he could stop behaving like a life support system for a hard-on.

"So when do you think I'll be ready for my next fight?" Jamie asked as she rested between sets.

"Got to break that bad habit of yours first," he reminded her.

"I know. Just…curious," she said.

"Impatient, you mean. Every fighter wants to rush to his next fight."

"*Her* next fight," she corrected, a gleam of humor in her eyes.

"Yeah, well, that's my bad habit," he admitted. "Got to keep reminding myself who I'm dealing with."

As if he needed reminding that she was a woman. His gaze dipped to her breasts. Man, but he wanted to taste her.

He was surprised by the intent look in her eyes when he returned his gaze to her face. She looked…hungry. Almost predatory.

His cock tightened as he understood that she'd caught him looking at her and knew that he was thinking about her.

And she liked it. A lot.

A bolt of pure desire shot through him.

Damn.

"You know what? You should just work your way 'round the machines," he said, standing. "I'm going to go for a run. I'll be back in an hour or so."

She frowned. "It's absolutely boiling outside."

"Yeah, I know."

Maybe all that baked-in heat in the roads and buildings would fry some of this lust out of his body. Something had to, because he'd never been so close to breaking his own rules and simply reaching out for what he wanted.

It was a quiet night thanks to the weather, but there were one or two guys still working out on the speedball and long bags in the other corner. He'd have to lead her through to his office and kick the door shut before he could get his hands on her. But once they were in there he could slide his hands inside those tight little pants she was wearing and find out if she was as hot and ready for him as he wanted her to be….

"You just keep doing your thing. And if you finish before I get back, I'll see you tomorrow," he said.

He walked away from her before he could act on his X-rated thoughts.

In the change room, he dragged on a pair of running shorts and a sports tank. When he laced his track shoes, he saw his hands were shaking.

This was getting out of control. He had to do something. Maybe give Kara another shot, force himself to go the distance this time. Surely once he actually had her in his bed, his body would report for duty?

Perversely hoping that it would be really, punishingly hot outside, he did some warm-up stretches and made his way to the front door.

"Hey, wait up," Jamie called from behind him.

He turned to see her approaching, her arms busy behind her head as she braided her hair.

"I need to get my roadwork hours up this week. I'll come with you," she said.

He stared at her. He'd tried to escape temptation, he really had. Now fate—or whatever—was throwing it right back in his face.

Every man had his breaking point. He had a feeling his was damn close.

"Sure, why not?" he said.

4

STUPID. Stupid. Stupid. Jamie chanted the mantra silently to herself as she pounded the pavement alongside Cooper.

Why had she gone out of her way to spend more time with him? Especially when they'd just had that moment where they'd looked into each other's eyes and acknowledged at last that there was some heavy-duty chemistry going on between them?

She'd been rejected by five other trainers before Cooper had reconsidered his original decision and taken her on. She wanted to prove to the sport, to herself and to her grandfather more than anything that she could make it to the top. So why was she risking all of that by pursuing her attraction to her trainer?

She shot a sideways glance at him as they ran, taking in his superbly fit body, the harsh, determined lines of his face, the confident ease of his movements.

Because he was hot, that was why. Because she wanted him. Because he'd started to invade her sleeping as well as her waking hours. Making beds at the hotel, she imagined him sprawled naked across the white sheets. Scrubbing down shower stalls, she pictured him beaded with water, pushing her up against the cool tiles as he took her. And at night she had the steamiest, dirtiest dreams she'd ever had about any man, dreams of hard heat and friction and need that left her gasping when she woke up alone and desperately horny.

She was seeing Dean tonight. Surely that would scratch this itch of curiosity and need that was currently driving her just a little bit crazy. She tried to picture Dean's face and body, tried to remember how good it had been between them last time… and couldn't get past her awareness of the man running at her side. The man who, for whatever reason, had quickly assumed center stage in her fantasy life.

Sweat dripped off her chin and onto her chest. She wiped her brow with her forearm. The smell of hot asphalt filled the air, and the only sound was the *slap slap* of their feet as they ran. Normal, sane people were taking refuge in their homes, curtains drawn, air-conditioning on. Not her and Cooper. They were punishing themselves in the heat.

He didn't want to want her. She didn't want to want him. But he did, and she did. And if Dean didn't do the trick tonight, Jamie honestly had no idea how to handle the situation. Human desire was a powerful, powerful thing. It had ruined marriages, brought down governments, destroyed dynasties. How in the hell was she supposed to stay strong when she saw the man *every day?* When he *touched* her time after time in the course of their work? When—

She caught movement out of the corners of her eyes and nearly groaned with frustration. He was peeling his tank top off, leaving his chest bare.

Oh boy, oh boy, oh boy.

She forgot to breathe for a moment as he balled his top in his hand and mopped his sweaty chest with it. He was beautiful. Great pecs, amazing abs, those big shoulders. Lucky she was already panting. As it was, she could barely keep her eyes off him, her gaze constantly darting to the side to keep checking that, yes, he really was that damned hot.

"So, do you miss it?" she blurted suddenly, desperate to normalize the situation. "Fighting, I mean."

He shrugged, his breath coming easily despite the fact they'd been running for nearly half an hour now.

"Of course. It's been the center of my world since I was sixteen years old. Never really known anything else."

"And you had to walk away from the title."

"No choice. Not if I didn't want to go blind," he said.

She tried to imagine how hard it must have been. To have worked like a dog to get to the top of the pile, only to have to give it all up because his body let him down.

"You must have been so pissed."

"For a while. What's done is done. No point wasting energy," he said. "I've got the gym now, my fighters. Life goes on."

Despite the surface confidence of his words, she heard the uncertainty beneath them. He was still feeling his way, trying to work out what life was about if it wasn't about the ring and winning and training and being the best.

"You're a great trainer," she said impulsively. She felt herself blush.

He shot her a look. "Suck-ups get an extra mile."

"I'm not sucking up, just telling it the way it is. All the guys are happy. Ray keeps saying that coming over to you was the smartest move he ever made."

He shrugged, but she could tell he was pleased. Hell, who didn't like to know they were doing a good job? He was big on praise. She'd noticed that about him over the past few days. He always rewarded hard work with a well-placed word or a pat on the shoulder or the back. She'd started to look forward to those moments, to seeing the light of approval in his eyes.

Another reason why sleeping with him would be a big mistake. She was well aware that there was a healthy dose of hero worship mixed in with her lust. He'd been a great champion. He was an inspiring trainer. Giving in to basic instinct would mess things up between them big-time.

Or…maybe it would clear the air.

The thought popped into her head as though it had been hand-delivered by the devil himself.

The road ahead began to rise, and Cooper pulled ahead of her as he dug deeper. She eyed his broad back and powerful legs greedily, toying with the idea that had just insinuated itself into her thoughts.

Hypothetically speaking, if they let instinct take over and went at each other, all the sexual tension that had been dogging her days would be gone. The weirdness between them would be a nonissue—for both of them. No hyperawareness, no waking fantasies, no nothing. Just…satisfaction. All the questions her body had been asking would be answered. They could put it behind them and move on.

The more she thought about it, the more she liked it. It made sense. She wasn't the kind of woman who had to dress sex up as something else to enjoy it—for her, it was simply two bodies seeking pleasure with each other. Most men, in her experience, were on the same wavelength and she'd heard enough gossip about Cooper and his women over the years to suspect that they shared a similar philosophy when it came to the bedroom.

In theory, there was nothing stopping them.

In no seconds flat, her body was on fire as she gave herself permission to experience her full desire for Cooper. As they neared the top of the hill, her anticipation rose and with it her heartbeat.

She was determined to have him now that she'd made her decision. First chance she got, she'd make her play, get this madness out of her system.

"You ready to head back?" he asked as they started down the hill.

It was past dusk, and they were about five minutes from the gym, running through the backstreets of Newtown. In a handful of moments, they'd have privacy. His office, the change rooms—she didn't care, as long as there was bare skin and heavy breathing involved.

"Absolutely," she said.

He shot her a look but didn't say anything. They completed the rest of their run in silence.

Usually after roadwork she felt pleasantly tired and warm and loose. Today, despite the heat, she was buzzing. She could feel her pulse pounding low in her belly and between her legs. Her mind was filled with steamy images as she anticipated his touch.

She'd been thinking about this from the moment she first saw him in the flesh, she finally admitted to herself. Weeks and weeks of secret wanting, all of it about to come to a head....

The coolness of the air-conditioned gym hit her the moment they pushed on the front doors. One of the gym attendants—Jason?—was tidying up the front counter.

"Good, you're back," he said, looking relieved. "I was a bit worried, since it was time to lock up."

Cooper frowned and looked at the time. It was twenty minutes past the usual closing.

"Sorry, mate, I didn't have my watch on. You head off, I'll lock up," he said.

"Yeah? Great. Thanks," Jason said, grabbing his car keys and heading for the door.

Jamie smiled to herself. Now they really were alone.

"I'll lock this for now. You can let yourself out when you're finished in the shower," Cooper said as he latched the front door after Jason.

She stepped in front of him when he turned to head for the change rooms, blocking his path.

His hair was damp with sweat, his chest glistening. She studied him for a few delicious seconds before meeting his questioning gaze.

"I think we have a problem," she said.

He frowned. "Do we?"

"Yeah. And I think the best way to take care of it is to just deal with it, get it out of our systems."

He frowned. She took a step closer and she saw something wild and exciting flare in the depths of his eyes.

"No. I'm your trainer, Jamie," he said—but he also took a deep breath, as though those careful words weren't his first impulse.

"Yep. And you want to sleep with me. Just like I want to sleep with you. I've been thinking about it all week," she said. "It makes it hard to concentrate. It's driving me crazy."

"Which is exactly why this isn't going to happen," Cooper said. "We're supposed to be getting you ready for your next fight."

He took a step around her. Jamie reached for the hem of her sports crop and pulled it over her head. Her breasts bounced free, her nipples already tight in anticipation of his touch.

"Damn," he said. His gaze caressed her, and his face was tight with restrained desire.

"Let's just do it, get it out of our systems and move on," she said.

Cooper closed his eyes, the muscles of his chest and arms tensing.

"It's my job to coach you, to advise you, to protect you. This will mess things up, Jamie," he said.

"No, it won't. It'll make it cleaner. No more wondering, no more imagining. It'll be a nonissue, over."

He opened his eyes. She could see the resolve harden in him.

"I'm not starting my training career by screwing one of my fighters," he said.

Frustration and need welled up inside her. She knew he wanted her as much as she wanted him. She was so sure that this was what they needed—the release of it, the freedom of it.

She took a last step forward, so close that she could feel the heat coming off his body, so close that her nipples brushed his chest.

"You're really going to let this go to waste?" she asked, holding his eye as she slid a hand onto the long, thick ridge straining against the fabric of his shorts.

He felt so big and hard in her hand she almost purred with anticipation.

His jaw tightened as she gripped him through his shorts and rubbed her hand up and down his shaft, once, twice, maintaining eye contact all the while.

He swore and reached for her, hauling her against him and angling her head as he took her mouth in a fierce, no-holds-barred kiss. She closed her eyes as she discovered his shoulders and arms with her free hand, the other remaining on his straining cock.

His tongue danced with hers, stroked it, teased it as his hands slid onto her breasts. She arched her back as he massaged them, plucking at her nipples before squeezing them gently. Between her thighs, molten heat pooled and she relinquished her grip on his erection in favor of grabbing his butt and grinding herself against him.

He felt so good. So strong and big and hard. His shoulders, his belly, his thighs, his cock…

She dropped her head back as he broke their kiss and began to lick and suck and bite his way down her neck, finally pulling first one then the other nipple into his mouth. His tongue was hot and fast as it flicked over and over her, and she clenched her hands into his taut butt and dragged him as close as they could possibly get with clothes on.

"Cooper…" she begged, needing more.

He responded by sucking her nipple so hard it almost hurt and sliding both hands down her back, beneath the waistband of her hot pants and over her butt cheeks. His hands massaged her curves for a torturous moment before he slid farther still and she felt the first magic touch of his fingers between her thighs.

"Oh, man," he groaned as he discovered how wet and hot she was for him.

She made an inarticulate, needy sound and widened her stance, inviting him in. Backing her up against the front counter, he slid a hand around her hip and down the front of her pants, into her damp curls. She held her breath as he slid a long finger between her folds, gliding in her slick heat, seeking the heart of her. Her whole body contracted as he found her and slid inside. She sobbed his name and reached for his hard-on again, moving her hands inside his running shorts to grip the pure, hardened steel of him.

He worked his hand between her thighs, his mouth busy at her breasts, his body tense and focused entirely on her. Then his thumb found her clitoris, and she bucked against him as he pressed her, teased her, flicked her.

She wanted him inside her when she came, but already her climax was rushing up at her, fast and furious, and all she could do was let it take her, her muscles throbbing around his clever fingers.

His touch gentled as the tension left her body, then he slid his hand free from between her thighs and lifted his head from her breasts. She stared at him, loving the dazed, unfocused look in his eyes, already imagining how good it was going to be between them when he was inside her.

She reached for the waistband of his running shorts, ready to strip him bare. He caught her hand.

"No."

"What?" she asked, not quite understanding the word.

"You heard me." His eyes were crisp and clear, not a shadow of doubt in sight. "That's as far as it can go, Jamie."

He had to be joking. They were just getting started. She still hadn't tasted him, or had him inside her. She hadn't discovered all the secret, soft places on his body that drove him wild. There was still too much unknown, unexplored…

"Cooper, forget your conscience for ten minutes. Hell, forget it for an hour or two. It's just sex. It doesn't mean anything, it won't change anything," she said.

She reached for him again. This time he caught her hand and held it loosely in his.

"Yeah, it will. We have a professional relationship. My job is to get the best out of you, not sleep with you. You're my *fighter,* Jamie. We're supposed to trust each other, not do each other."

She stared at him, unable to believe that he could walk away from all the heat between them. She could see how much he wanted her still—his hard-on was damned unmissable the way it tented the front of his shorts.

"Let me put it this way—what do you need more, someone in your bed, or a trainer?" he asked.

That hit her like a bucket of cold water. He'd drawn a line, given her a choice. And despite how much her body craved his touch, no matter how much her blood sang with need for him, she knew and he knew which option she was going to choose.

"Fine," she said.

It had been a long time since a man had said no to her. Not that she thought she was some irresistible femme fatale or anything, but she'd never gotten half-naked with a man and had him walk away.

How very bloody noble and self-controlled of Cooper.

It made her want to punch him, a good jab straight to his rock-hard belly. Probably it would hurt her more than it would hurt him, but it might relieve some of the frustration she was feeling.

"I suppose I should thank you for saving me from myself," she said.

Cooper remained impassive.

"I'd better not catch you looking at me again," she said. "If I catch one hint that you're thinking of anything below the neckline…"

To her intense annoyance, he smiled.

"Yeah? What are you going to do?" he asked.

She glared at him, knowing he was right. What *was* she going to do? *Force* him to sleep with her? Quit?

Bang her head against a brick wall?

Damn him. Damn him and her stupid hormones or phero-mones or whatever was responsible for how she felt right now.

Without another word, she turned on her heel and headed for the change room.

"Jamie."

She turned around. He tossed her crop top at her. She caught it with one hand.

"For what it's worth, you're the hottest damn thing I've ever said no to," he said.

What was she supposed to say to that?

She flipped him the finger.

"Thanks a lot," she said.

IF THE POPE didn't announce Cooper's sainthood soon, there was no justice in the world. Cooper watched Jamie walk away, naked except for those teeny tiny hot pants and her running shoes.

She was magnificent. And he'd just said no to her.

The moment she entered the women's change room, he let his shoulders sag and ran a hand through his hair.

He still couldn't quite believe that he'd said no to her. He had a boner in his pants that couldn't quite believe it, either.

She'd felt so good in his arms. Even her sweat had tasted good, clean and fresh. And the needy sound she'd made when he suckled her breasts, and the way her muscles had clenched around him when he slid his finger inside her… He was going to be tortured by those few breathless moments for the rest of his life, along with all the what-ifs.

What if he'd taken what she was offering?

What if he'd lifted her onto that counter and wrapped her legs around his waist and buried himself to the hilt inside her?

Shaking his head, he derailed his thoughts before his cock literally exploded with frustrated desire. Then, feeling like a desperate fourteen-year-old, he took himself off to the change room and took care of business solo, with nothing but the hot flow of the shower and a handful of soap for company.

Not quite the same as all the slippery sweet heat that Jamie had been offering. Not even close, in fact.

But it was going to have to do. He'd made a commitment to her, and he was going to stand by it if it killed him.

She was gone by the time he'd dried himself off and dressed, not that he'd expected anything different. He paused by the front counter to switch on the after-hours answering machine. He would never be able to enter his gym again without remembering Jamie pushed up against the counter, her body straining with desire as she found her climax.

He'd looked into her face as it gripped her, wanting to see her lose control, loving the way her mouth had opened, the way she'd panted, the little frown she'd gotten between her eyebrows. He'd never done that with a woman before. He'd prided himself on making sure they had a good time, but he'd never savored a woman's pleasure so much before.

Get over it. She's a hot body, a challenge and off-limits. Of course you want to screw her. You've spent your life bucking the system.

But at the end of the day, she was just a woman, same as any other woman that he'd slept with. Or not slept with, to be technically correct. There was nothing special about any of it.

As LUCK WOULD HAVE IT, Arthur Holloway accompanied Jamie to the gym for her workout the next day. Even though Cooper told himself that he and Jamie were grown adults and that nothing had happened last night for either of them to feel uncomfortable about, he still felt a flicker of guilt when he met the other man's eyes. There was just something about the old guy, a sort of calm, centered integrity, that made Cooper feel like an asshole for what had almost happened.

Cooper had had two trainers during his career, both of whom still occupied important roles in his life. A legend in fighting circles, Harry Muldoon had spotted Cooper brawling in the street when he was sixteen years old and homeless and shaped him from nothing. Harry had been everything to Cooper for many years—father, brother, teacher, trainer. When he retired, Cooper had felt like a heel going to another trainer. It had taken him a long time to forge a bond with Vaughn Stevenson, his second and last trainer. Younger and better-educated than Harry, Vaughn had brought fresh ideas and new science to Cooper's training regime. But Cooper had trusted both men implicitly—with his health, his career, his money, even his life, if need be.

That was the kind of trust he wanted his fighters to place in him. He was pretty sure he had the goods, experience and knowledge, to become the sort of trainer he wanted to be. But what had happened with Jamie last night had shaken his sense of his own values.

She had to be able to trust him, and he had to be able to make clear-headed decisions about her. Sex was not, and never could be, a part of that equation.

"She's looking good," Arthur said when Cooper finally forced himself to cross the gym to check in on Jamie's workout.

"Yeah," Cooper said, watching Jamie's form as she went at the speedball.

She staunchly ignored him. He didn't force the issue. The old man slid a sideways look his way, sensing something was up. Cooper fought the urge to shuffle his feet.

"She's been working pretty hard. Wants to impress you," Arthur said. "Even blew off her date last night so she could get up early and do some more roadwork."

Cooper tried not to let his interest show on his face. Jamie had had a date last night? He remembered her mentioning a 'friend' whom she planned to meet at nine after her workout. Only, according to Arthur, she hadn't.

Because of what had happened between them?

"I'm already impressed. Jamie's got a lot of natural talent," he said.

"It's in the blood," Arthur said. "She practically grew up in the ring."

"Yeah?" Cooper cocked his head, silently inviting more information. It hadn't really occurred to him before, but Jamie never said much about her family or her life. He knew she worked as a maid at one of the big hotels in the city. He knew she lived with her grandfather. But that was pretty much it.

Either Arthur didn't pick up on his silent cue, or he was avoiding responding. Frowning, Cooper remembered that when he'd asked the old guy about his fighting record he'd clammed up, too.

"So the whole family was involved in the sport, then?" Cooper asked.

Arthur shoved his hands into the pockets of his Bermuda shorts and ducked his chin into his chest.

"Yeah, guess you could say that," he said. "Sure is hot outside, eh?"

Cooper ignored the change of subject.

"You never did say where you did most of your fighting, Arthur. By the looks of you I guess you were a heavyweight?" he asked.

"For a while, but then I dropped down to cruiserweight. And mostly I fought in the States," Arthur said. "They say there's a cool front coming through tonight, did you hear?"

"That'd put you over there when Ali and Frazier were around. You ever see the great man fight?" Cooper asked, genuinely interested. There wasn't a fighter alive who didn't admire Muhammad Ali and envy him his career.

"*See* him? Went seven rounds with him in Louisville, Kentucky, one time," Arthur said, his eyes bright and his shoulders back as he puffed his chest out. "That man could move, let me tell you. Like poetry in motion."

Cooper narrowed his eyes. "You fought Muhammad Ali?"

He wasn't calling the old guy a liar, but he was pretty sure he'd never heard of an Arthur Holloway taking on Ali.

Arthur blushed, the tide of color racing up from his collar 'til even the top of his head was pink. "Sparring match," he said. "Just fooling around, you know."

"Right. Sure," Cooper said.

"Might go get myself some water," Arthur said, heading for the front counter.

Cooper stared after him. He felt embarrassed for the old guy. If a fighter was going to brag about a fight he never fought, he should know better than to pick the most famous boxer in history.

When he brought his attention back to Jamie, she was watching him, her expression unreadable.

"Feeling virtuous, Mr. Self-Control?" she asked after a few tense minutes of silence.

"Ever heard of letting sleeping dogs lie?"

"I don't see what the big deal is," she said. "I'm not into all that hearts and flowers crap, if that's what you're worried about. Love is for greeting card manufacturers, and I don't ever want to get married and have kids, so that pretty much lets you off the hook on all fronts."

"Except professionally," he said, crossing his arms over his chest.

She took a few last shots at the speedball, her bottom lip decidedly pouty. She was sulking.

Despite himself, he was flattered.

"Hey, for all you know I could be hung like a hamster and it would all be over in five seconds flat," he said.

Was he *insane,* or did he actually just run down his own sexual performance to an incredibly hot woman?

She rolled her eyes. "*Puh-lease,* you think I'm feeling impaired? I had my hands on you last night, I know what you're packing. I know *exactly* what I'm missing out on."

Damn, now *he* was blushing. Rubbing the back of his neck with his hand, he glanced at her and found she was laughing at him with her eyes.

"Don't worry, I get it," she said. "I just wanted to give you a hard time."

Hard being the operative word.

"Thanks. I appreciate it."

"My pleasure. And I mean that," she said.

"Just for that, you can drop and give me fifty push-ups," he said.

She raised an eyebrow at him, then hit the mat and started counting them off.

Man, she was a piece of work. He couldn't help but admire her courage. Her frank and open attitude to sex was hot, and her straight-down-the-line way of handling the world was just plain likeable.

She was likeable. Under different circumstances, at a different time…

He frowned. Even if he did allow himself to sleep with Jamie, her likeability or not wouldn't make any difference to the outcome. He'd never had a relationship with any woman that lasted longer than a few months. His career meant he moved around a lot. Plus he'd been exposed to a lot of gorgeous women who were more than happy to have sex with him, no strings attached. There had never been a lot of incentive to commit himself to one woman before.

But life was a little different these days. He was enjoying not having to travel around as much. He had a great house in Annandale, a couple of minutes' drive from the gym, and when he wasn't itching to be back in the ring, he was enjoying spending more time with his friends and less time training. Who was to say that his attitude toward women wasn't changing as well?

All of which was irrelevant where Jamie was concerned, he reminded himself as she counted off the last push-up and rolled onto her back to catch her breath.

"You're a real hard-ass. And I can vouch for that," she said, wiggling her eyebrows at him suggestively.

He told her to clock some time on the long bag before

walking away. Only then did he let himself smile. She had lip to spare, that was for sure.

That night, he made his way over to Ray Marshall's place for dinner with a couple of old boxing buddies. It was a boys' night, and the beer and language flowed thick and fast as they talked bull. Like Ray, the other two guys, Tom and Marco, were still actively fighting, and Cooper felt a distinct pang of envy when he heard them discussing their upcoming bouts and talking about cutting weight and training schedules.

Gotta get over that, he told himself as he made his way to the bathroom in between courses. *No point wanting something you can never have.*

It wasn't as though he wasn't enjoying his new role as trainer. He'd been surprised by how satisfying he found it, in fact. It wasn't the same as being the king of the ring, but he was beginning to appreciate the benefits of shaping someone else's career, the satisfaction of helping someone else achieve their goals. He was good at it, too. Pretty soon, his gym was going to be attracting talent from all over.

His life wasn't over. Not by a long shot.

Like the rest of the house, Ray's bathroom was large and modern, although he'd personalized it with some boxing memorabilia. After washing his hands, Cooper stopped to admire a Muhammad Ali poster, a montage of classic images from the great man's career alongside his complete fight history.

It made him think of Arthur Holloway's boast that he'd fought Ali, and the way the old man had colored when Cooper had called him on it. Man, talk about an awkward moment.

He was about to turn away and rejoin Ray and the other guys when he caught sight of a name on the fight record: Arthur Sawyer. He'd fought Ali in Louisville, Kentucky, in 1961.

His gut tightened as he stared at the simple line of text.

Again he remembered the flush of color rising up Arthur's neck and face that afternoon. He remembered the old man's evasiveness when it came to talking about himself or his family. Then he remembered the way Ray had looked uncomfortable when he first introduced Jamie to him, all those months ago out by the pool.

See *him? Went seven rounds with him in Louisville, Kentucky, one time.* Jesus, he could still hear the pride in the old guy's voice.

Cooper swore under his breath.

He hadn't caught Arthur lying about his fighting record— the old man had been busted lying about something much more fundamental: his identity. Because while the world had never heard of Arthur Holloway, Arthur Sawyer was a legend of Australian boxing—surpassed only by his son, Jack Sawyer, who had held the heavyweight championship title for an impressive five years before he retired, only to return for an ill-fated comeback that resulted in him being charged with fraud for throwing a fight. He'd taken his own life a few years back, after being ostracized by the boxing community, and had instantly become as infamous as he'd once been famous.

Jamie had lied to him.

She'd lied to him right from the word go.

5

JAMIE PROPPED HER FEET on the coffee table and dipped her spoon into the container of low-fat vanilla yogurt she'd allowed herself as a treat instead of having sex with Cooper. It wasn't quite ice cream or chocolate. In fact, it almost tasted *healthy,* which was a sure sign it wasn't doing it for her in the food-as-consolation stakes. More the pity, since she wasn't going to get a shot at either of her two favorite poisons—or Cooper, for that matter—anytime soon.

The flickering light from the muted TV sent shadows up the wall. She stared restlessly at the screen as she dug into the yogurt. It had been a while since she'd been home on her own. Her grandfather usually went to play seniors poker on Friday nights. Typically she'd go out, too. She didn't have a lot of friends, but those that she did have were close—Ray, Narelle, a couple of guys from Tae Kwon Do. But she hadn't felt like playing with any of them this evening.

Dropping her spoon into the empty container, Jamie leaned forward to dump it on the coffee table. There was nothing on TV, she'd never been a big reader and she'd already sucked the life out of her grandfather's most recent copy of *The Ring*.

Closing her eyes, she indulged in her favorite pastime: imagining the moment when she stood center ring with the women's world middleweight boxing championship belt in her hands. She could almost feel the magic of the moment. All the sacrifices would have paid off, and the past would be obliterated.

People would remember what the Sawyer name stood for in boxing. Her grandfather could hold his head high again. Her promise to him would be fulfilled. And the lump of anger and hurt and guilt that had been sitting on her chest for the past two years would be gone.

She almost leaped out of her skin when someone pounded on the front door. The security chain rattled with the force of the blow and she stood warily. She and her grandfather lived close to the city in Glebe—the seedy, down-at-heel part, not the expensive, double-income-no-kids part—and there'd been trouble in their apartment building before. Kids chroming and doing other drugs, alcoholics on benders.

She checked through the peephole and frowned when she saw the hard lines of Cooper's angry face.

What was he doing there? She shot a glance over her shoulder, acutely aware of how low-rent her apartment was compared to everything he owned. She shut down the thought immediately. So, she didn't have a lot of money. She had nothing to be ashamed of.

"Is something wrong?" she asked as she opened the door.

Cooper gave here a cold look and pushed past her into the apartment.

"You lied to me," he said.

She didn't even bother trying to cover—he knew who she really was. She could tell by how angry he was.

"I didn't think it was relevant?" she said.

"You didn't think your real name was relevant," he said. "Jamie *Sawyer*, daughter of Jack *Sawyer*, granddaughter of Arthur *Sawyer*. You didn't think your boxing trainer might find that pedigree even vaguely interesting?"

"I didn't think it mattered," she said.

"Bullshit. If it hadn't mattered, you wouldn't have lied."

She couldn't meet his eye. "I didn't want people to know. Not until I had a few fights under my belt."

Or maybe a world title.

"Yeah, well, that was a decision we should have made together. But there's no point chewing the air over it. I just came over to let you know we're done. You're no longer welcome in my gym," he said.

The bottom dropped out of her stomach.

"What?"

"This—" he gestured between the two of them "—relationship is supposed to be about trust. Me to you, you to me. You lied to me. You withheld important information. I can't work with that."

He headed for the door. She couldn't believe what he'd said, that he was going to dump his decision on her that way and leave.

"No. Wait," she said, darting forward to block his path. "At least give me a chance to explain."

"I don't care. I don't want to hear excuses. This was a mistake."

She didn't move. "I'm not letting you go until you at least hear me out," she said.

Panic surged inside her. It had been so hard to get Cooper to take her on, and everything had been falling into place with him. But now she'd blown it and he wasn't even going to give her a chance to put things right.

"Do you mind stepping away from the door?" he asked, his jaw tensing.

"Let me explain," she insisted.

He moved forward, and she did the first thing that came to mind—she squared up and punched him in the chest.

There was a moment of stunned silence.

"Right, that's it," he said, grabbing her wrists.

She wrenched away from him when he tried to haul her out of the way, bracing her legs, putting all she had into it. His grip was unbreakable. Panting, she glared at him.

"You think you know everything, that everything's so cut and dried. *You* try living with the legacy of Jack Sawyer hanging over you. *You* try watching your grandfather fade a little more each day as everything he values turns to shit and his friends turn their backs on him and he's left with nothing."

She gestured with her head toward her grandfather's armchair.

"That old man is the bravest, most honorable, most generous person in the world. All I wanted was to give him back what my father took away from us five years ago when he sold his career for a few thousand dollars."

Angry, desperate tears stung her eyes. She blinked furiously but she couldn't stop them from falling. She twisted her face away and yanked on her wrists again. She never cried in front of anyone, ever.

"Could you let me go, please?" she asked in a low, intense tone.

He released her. She dashed the back of her hand across her eyes and swung around to open the door.

"Go," she said, not looking at him.

She strode across the room and into the small hallway that led to the bedrooms. In the privacy of her room, she sat on the bed, her back to the door.

Her hands clenched into fists, she pressed her knuckles against her forehead. Crying was such a weak, pointless exercise. It didn't change anything, it just signaled to the world that a person was down and vulnerable and ready to be exploited.

She would find another trainer. Or she would continue with what Cooper had started. Either way, it didn't matter. This wasn't over. She was nowhere near ready to give up.

Her shoulders started to shudder as a sob rose in her throat.

She'd been fighting for so long—ever since her father's betrayal had become a public scandal. Five years. Fighting to keep him out of jail for a year, then fighting to save their home and their savings while he was doing two long years for fraud. And, finally, fighting to keep her grandfather alive after her father had compounded his crimes by killing himself.

"Jamie."

Cooper was still here. Gulping, she swiped at her tears and kept her back to him.

"Get out. You wanted to go, so do it," she said, her voice cracking.

The mattress sank as he sat on the end of the bed and she shot to her feet.

"For God's sake, will you just go?" she said.

He watched her, his expression unreadable.

"Explain it to me," he said quietly.

She stared at him for a beat before she got it.

"Oh, right. I cried a bit, and you feel sorry for me now. Well, you know what you can do with your pity? You can take it and shove it up your—"

"I don't feel sorry for you," he said, talking over her. "You're a pain in the ass, you irritate the hell out of me, but the last thing I feel for you is pity."

She frowned, thrown.

"Sit and talk to me. Tell me what I'm up against," he said.

"You're not *up against* anything," she said. "Don't try to make me sound like a head case."

"Anything that messes with a fighter's mindset is a problem," he said. "I don't want you thinking about anything except hurting your opponent when you're in that ring."

Maybe it was the way he said it, as though she was still his fighter and he her trainer. Or maybe it was the steadiness of his regard. Or maybe she simply wanted to say it out loud, she'd been holding it all inside for so long.

Sitting, she started to talk.

"My grandfather had a major heart attack six months ago. He'd been not great for a while before that, ever since Jack… Anyway, he nearly died. The doctors didn't give him much of a chance. He'd been so worn down by everything. After Jack's fraud case, we had so many legal bills. We had to sell the house, the car, everything. And all of Grandpa's old boxing buddies turned their backs on us. What my father did, throwing that match…he shamed so many people. He made it all a lie, his whole career, my grandfather's career. And then he didn't even have the courage to face up to what he'd done. He'd been out of prison one week when he killed himself. Grandpa found his body…."

She paused to suck in some air. Cooper waited her out, a silent presence at the end of the bed.

"When he got sick, I knew Grandpa didn't feel as though there was anything to live for. He'd been so tapped out. He used to walk into his old gym up in Queensland and everyone would stop what they were doing to talk to him, just to look at him. He was a living legend, you know? But after Jack, people turned on him—he was no one, nothing. I wanted to give that back to him. So I made him a promise."

Jamie paused, remembering the muffled quiet of the hospital room, the rhythmic swish of the ventilator, the pitying looks of the nursing staff. For the first time in her life she'd held her grandfather's hand in her own and felt the frailty of his old bones. He'd always seemed so big to her, larger than life.

"I made a promise that I would change things. That I would get back his respect for him. That I would make people forget what Jack had done," she said. "He woke up the next day. And he's been better every day since I started training for the ring."

There was a long silence as Cooper processed her words.

"You're doing all this for your grandfather?" he asked. "There's a lot of pain waiting for you out in that ring, Jamie. Fighting for someone else isn't enough."

"I'm doing it for me, too," she said in a low tone. "I'm a Sawyer, too. I don't want my father to be the measure of all of us. I hate him for what he did."

She'd never said it out loud, but it was true. She'd looked up to him, idolized him, and he'd sold his reputation for money he didn't need. He'd betrayed them all then committed the ultimate betrayal by taking his own life and leaving them to clean up the mess.

The mattress dipped as Cooper moved closer. The warm weight of his hand landed in the middle of her back. She realized she was crying again, the tears leaking from her eyes and dripping off her nose and chin and onto her clenched hands.

"I never cry," she hiccupped.

He didn't say anything, just rubbed comforting circles on her back until the tears stopped and she started sniffing. He shifted then, pulling something from his pocket—a handkerchief.

A bubble of laughter rose inside her.

"You're kidding, right? Big bad Cooper Fitzgerald packs a hanky?" she said, her voice husky from crying.

"It's about to save your ass, isn't it?" He tipped her chin up with one hand and wiped at her tears with the other.

She let him, mostly because he was bigger than she was and she wasn't up to fighting him. But her gaze slid away from his. She had no idea what he was thinking or feeling right now. She hated being so exposed and vulnerable.

"Blow," he said, holding the handkerchief beneath her nose.

She took the handkerchief from his hand, not about to let him blow her nose like a little kid. Once she'd finished, she shifted awkwardly, not sure what would happen next.

"I'll wash this for you," she said, indicating the scrunched-up handkerchief.

He shrugged. "That's usually the way it works."

"I suppose I look like one of those goldfish with freaky puffy eyes," she said.

He didn't respond.

God, what had she told him?

Everything.

And she'd bawled like a little kid.

"I guess this is why you wanted to stick to male boxers, huh?" She twisted the handkerchief in her hands.

"You can't fight all the time, Jamie," he said.

"What's that supposed to mean?" she asked, even though she knew.

"It means it's okay to let your guard down every now and then," he said. "You think I don't have bad days? Ray? The other guys at the gym? Almost anyone who gets in that ring has got some kind of monkey on their back. Who else would volunteer for all that pain?"

"What's yours, then?" she challenged, not prepared to take his get-out-of-jail-free card. Last time she'd trusted a man, last time she'd made herself vulnerable, she'd been taught a lesson she wouldn't forget in a long, long time.

"I lived on the streets for four years until Harry Muldoon spotted me when I was sixteen."

She stilled. She hadn't been expecting that. Homeless... On the streets at the age of twelve...

Slowly, she lifted her head and met his gaze.

"Like I said, everyone's got a monkey on their back," he said.

She wanted to ask more questions, but she didn't. He had offered her a quid pro quo to even the confessional score, not an invitation to pry into his personal history.

"Thank you."

He nodded. Then he stood. She felt a clutch of something— need? fear? desperation?—in her chest when she looked up at him. He was going?

"You going to be okay?" he asked.

Jamie stood. She didn't want him to leave. She'd just bared her soul to him. She didn't want to be alone. She didn't want him to walk out the door and to never see him again.

"Don't go," she said.

Instantly the air crackled with awareness as he looked into her face. His gaze dropped to her lips, then lower, to her breasts. That quickly, her heart shifted into overdrive and her blood turned thick as treacle. Without waiting for him to say what he always said—no—she stuck her thumbs into the waistband of her workout pants. She peeled them over her hips and butt and down her legs in one move, taking her panties with them. Then she whipped her T-shirt over her head and unclipped her bra. When she was naked, she moved closer to him, pressing herself against him. She could see a telltale pulse hammering at the base of his neck, could feel the tension in his body.

"Don't go," she repeated. She took his left hand in both of hers and placed it against her sternum. She locked eyes with him as she slid his hand down onto her breast. Her whole body tightened in response. She continued to push his hand down, down, over her ribs and belly and down between her legs. Her own hands curving around his single big hand, she guided him between her thighs to where she was wet and ready for him.

"I am not a freakin' saint." He growled the words.

But he didn't try to pull his hand away.

"I don't want you to be," she whispered. Then she curled a leg around the back of his knee and leaned back with her body weight to tumble him onto her bed.

He could have easily resisted. He didn't. His body fell on top of hers as they hit the mattress, and she closed her eyes as she felt the glorious pressure of his hard chest against her breasts.

He was still for a moment, then he let his breath out on a sigh. She waited for him to explode into action the way he had last time when his control had snapped, but he turned his face into her neck and opened his mouth and began to kiss her. He'd pulled his hand from between her legs when they fell, instinctively trying to break their fall, and now he slid both hands up the sides of her body until they were splayed wide just beneath her breasts. He held her that way for a few long seconds as he made a leisurely survey of the side of her neck with his mouth and tongue. Sensation unfurled in her belly, warm and liquid.

They were going to take this slow, not fast and crazy like last time. Part of her welcomed the thought, even as part of her rebelled, wanting—needing—the oblivion of hard, hot sex to blot out what had just happened between them.

Sensation quickly washed all thought away as he slid his hands up onto her breasts and began to massage them, his fingers playing her nipples, his palms cupping her weight. She closed her eyes and groaned low in her throat, spreading her legs beneath him so that he nestled more snugly into the cradle of her thighs. The scrape of his jeans against her naked skin was highly erotic, and she circled her hips, savoring the friction, reveling in the feel of his erection pressing against her through the denim.

Slowly he trailed open-mouthed kisses up her neck, and her whole body shuddered as he slid his tongue into her ear. She moaned, her back arching. When had her ears ever been so sensitive? But she felt like every part of her body was on fire when Cooper was touching her.

Her own hands were clutching his shoulders, holding him steady, or perhaps simply holding him. She didn't want him to go, to leave her wanting again. This time, she had to have him.

She felt the rasp of his five o'clock shadow as he dragged his mouth from her ear. She opened her lips in anticipation as his mouth finally found hers. His tongue slid inside and she stroked it with her own, desire rippling through her body in powerful, building waves.

She began to move her hands, gliding them down his back, one finding his butt, the other tugging his shirt free from his jeans so she could touch his skin. She pressed her palm flat against the muscles of his waist, reveling in the leashed power she could feel beneath her hand.

One of his hands drifted from her breast to cup her butt. Lifting her, he silently encouraged her closer to him. She willingly pressed herself against him, her thighs wide, her body quivering.

"You are unbelievable," Cooper whispered into her mouth. "You make me so hot."

She reached for the hem of his shirt and began to tug it up

his back. He broke their kiss for a few, torturous seconds to shrug the shirt off entirely. Then his naked skin was against hers. She raked her hands down his back and opened her mouth wide to his invading kisses.

When had kissing ever been so intense, so amazing, so all-encompassing? She felt as though her bones had melted, as though everything inside her had become one big liquid ache.

Cooper ended their kiss and rolled to one side. She lay with her eyes half-closed, listening to the sound of denim sliding over skin, her breathing more and more shallow as she anticipated what was going to happen next. Him inside her, at last….

"Come here," he murmured. He reached out to draw her close again. Her legs tangled with his, their hips and chests coming together as they lay on their sides facing each other. He nudged a knee between her legs, encouraging her thighs apart. She smoothed a hand down his beautiful chest and belly until she felt the brush of his erection against her hand.

Wrapping her palm around him, she skimmed her hand up his shaft until she felt the hot velvet of the head of his cock. He was so thick and long. She ran her thumb back and forth across his head, imagining how it was going to feel to have all this masculinity pounding into her….

She felt his body tense, and he deepened their kiss for a few seconds before rolling on top of her. As he settled between her thighs, she guided his hardness to her softness. She rubbed herself against him, back and forth, back and forth, a torturous, silken, slippery tease.

Cooper nuzzled her neck, then he lowered his head to her breasts and began to lave her nipples with his tongue. The ache between her thighs became almost painful as her desire built. She sent a questing hand for the drawer beside her bed.

"Cooper," she said when she found a single small foil packet. He took it from her, levering himself on one elbow as he rolled on the condom. Watching him touch himself, stroking the latex on was one of the biggest turn-ons of her life.

Once he was satisfied they were protected, he stared down at her, his gaze smoky as it catalogued her straining breasts, her widely spread thighs, the neat strip of dark curly hair between them. Taking himself in hand, he positioned himself at her entrance, then lifted his gaze to hers and slowly flexed his hips.

She wanted to close her eyes and enjoy the first delicious stretch of him as he slid inside her, but his eyes compelled her to watch him, to share the moment. She bit her lip as he slowly, slowly buried himself to the hilt.

"You're so tight," he said, his voice low, his eyes closing as he felt her embrace him.

She tilted her hips and wrapped her legs around his and reveled in being so utterly, completely full.

He began to move, his big cock so hard, so right inside her, his butt flexing beneath her hands, his whole body straining. He kept the pace slow, building the friction between them, his strokes firm and knowing. She rode with him, matching her rhythm to his, desire coiling tighter and tighter inside her.

He lowered his head to her breasts again, his touch more demanding now, his mouth suckling, his teeth nipping, his hands shaping her. It was exactly what she wanted, what she needed. She dug her fingers into his butt and encouraged him to go harder, faster.

He lifted the pace, pounding into her now, the exquisite friction between them building, building… She threw her head back, her whole body trembling with tension as she felt her desire climb higher. And then she was shuddering around him, her hands clutching at him, her inner muscles pulsating, her breath coming in short, desperate pants as she came and came and came.

He slowed his strokes as her climax dissipated, withdrawing until he'd almost left her entirely before slowly plunging all the way back inside. She murmured her appreciation, rocking against him, her body warm and loose and damp. He licked at her breasts, teasing her nipples lightly, then gently sucking them into the heat of his mouth where he soothed his tongue over and over them. She rolled her head from side to side, her eyes closed, her hands busy mapping the muscles of his back and shoulders and butt.

He slid a hand down her belly, delving into her curls, finding the hard nub of her clitoris. Her eyes shot open as he pressed it, circled it, flicked it. Desire instantly flared to life inside her again.

Seeing the new awareness in her eyes, he grinned—a deeply satisfied, knowing grin.

"Let's see how you handle round two."

SHE WAS SO TIGHT and hot and wet, he couldn't believe that he'd lasted as long as he had. At the same time, he wanted to extend the pleasure as far as it would go. She was incredible, utterly uninhibited, her body the sexiest damn thing he'd ever had his hands on.

When she'd come, he'd almost lost it, he'd gotten off on her pleasure so much. The way she'd arched her back, the little hitch she'd gotten in her breathing, the way her fingers had curled into his butt and anchored him inside her as she shuddered around him…

Staring into her flushed face, taking in the tight peaks of her breasts, still wet from where he'd kissed them, admiring the flat planes of her stomach, he felt himself start to lose control. He couldn't last much longer, but he wanted to make sure she came with him. Shifting himself higher, he changed the angle of his strokes and slid his finger over and over her clit. She started to moan. She began to buck. He ground himself into her, reveling in her, giving himself up to the tension inside as he drove into her. So sweet, so tight, so wet, so open and willing… His whole body tensed as he climaxed, and beneath him Jamie tensed as she came a second time.

His body slick with sweat, he collapsed on top of her, aware of the pounding of her heart beneath him and the rapid rise and fall of both their chests. After a few minutes, he rolled to one side. He'd noticed a closed door when he came after her earlier. He stood and went in search of the bathroom. After taking care of business, he returned to the bedroom to find Jamie lying exactly as he'd left her, her eyelids at half-mast, her hair dark and tousled on the sheets.

He wasn't quite sure what to say. He'd expected sex with her to be good, especially considering the days and days of build-up to this moment. He hadn't expected it to be so intense and gripping and overwhelming.

She was a very attractive woman, in more ways than the physical. Watching her try to hold back her emotions when she'd been talking about her father and her grandfather... She'd hated crying in front of him, a true warrior to the end. Seeing her emotions leak out around her self-control had been painful to watch. He'd wanted to pull her into his arms and let her know it was all going to be all right.

Not an urge that had ever gripped him with any of the women he'd slept with previously. Not something he could guarantee for her, either.

The sheets rustled as she lifted herself up onto her elbows.

"My grandfather's going to be home soon," she said.

He blinked. She wanted him to go.

"Sure," he said, frowning.

He'd shucked his jeans and boxers in one move, and he pulled his underwear free and tugged it on, quickly following with his jeans. She passed him his shirt when he started buckling his belt. He shrugged into it and did up the minimum of buttons before sliding his feet into his shoes.

"Before you go—you're still going to be my trainer, right?" Jamie asked.

He stared at her. So beautiful, so determined, so goddamned

focused on redeeming herself and her family name. Was he the only one who had felt anything apart from a bunch of great sensory shit when they'd been together just now?

Feeling angry with her all of a sudden, he headed for the door.

"Is that a no?" she asked.

He paused in the doorway. "We need to sort some things out," he said.

A slow smile spread across her face.

"But you're still my trainer."

He stared at her for a long beat. "I'll see you tomorrow at the gym."

6

THE NEXT MORNING Cooper was doing paperwork in his office at the gym when Ray stuck his head in.

"Hey. Just wanted to see how it went with Jimmy."

Cooper had bailed on Ray's dinner party to go confront Jamie last night, and the other man was well aware of his reasons for leaving early. Cooper regarded him silently for a moment.

Ray had lied to him about Jamie. Which meant he had two fighters who had been dishonest with him.

"For what it's worth, I'm sorry. Jimmy and I go a long way back. She didn't want anyone to know, and I figured that was her decision," Ray said, tackling the issue head-on.

It was an apology, but there was a fair share of defiance in there, too, in the set of Ray's shoulders and the way he held Cooper's eye.

Fair enough. Cooper figured he'd probably feel about the same way if he were in Ray's shoes. He'd only known Jamie for a handful of weeks and already she'd burrowed into his psyche. It was clear to him that Ray was still half-gone on her—he would have found it almost impossible to deny Jamie if she came to him asking for help.

"Let's forget it, okay? Jamie and I have got some shit to sort out, but you and I are square. I get why you did it," Cooper said.

Ray came fully into the office.

"So it went okay last night, then?"

It was Cooper's turn to feel uncomfortable. "Like I said, we still have some shit to sort out."

Ray dropped into the chair opposite Cooper's desk. "Don't be too hard on her. She's copped a lot of crap in her life. All that stuff with her old man throwing that fight, then Kyle Vandenburg did her over, then her father's death… Is it any wonder she wanted to just put it all behind her?" Ray said.

"What's Kyle Vandenburg got to do with anything?"

A heavyweight, Kyle was the kind of egomaniacal moron who gave boxing a bad name. He brawled in bars, threw his weight around and hung with all the wrong people. He was also a dirty fighter. Cooper had beaten him twice in his career, and both times it had been a pleasure to pound the bastard into submission.

"He was hooked up with Jack for a while. Sort of a mentor thing. Jack toyed with training for a bit before he came out of retirement and took that last fight," Ray said. They both knew how that had ended—Jack had hit the canvas in round five after a lackluster display. He'd been arrested in the change room for fraud straight afterward, the unusual level of betting against him having tipped the authorities off. It had been front page news in the U.S. and Australia and had brought the sport an intense amount of scrutiny for several months afterward.

"When Jack went down on the fraud charges, Jimmy was stuck with a bunch of legal bills. Vandenburg stepped in to help out. Jimmy was only twenty-two. Just a kid. I mean, I knew her back then, and she was gorgeous, but there was no way I would have gone there. She was so upset about Jack, her and Arthur were really struggling. But Vandenburg didn't give a crap about any of that. He wanted her, and he got her. Told her he'd take care of everything, get his business manager involved to help them work things out."

Cooper rubbed the bridge of his nose. "Vandenburg ripped her off?" he asked.

Ray nodded. "Him and his business manager. The Sawyers

lost their house, cars, everything. Had to drop the appeal on Jack's sentence, and Jack wound up doing the full two years. Jimmy blamed herself for a long time for being such a soft touch. That's why she never lets her guard down any more. That asshole really did her good. Then her father finished the job two years ago when he killed himself."

Cooper remembered the way she'd hunched her shoulders in on herself last night as she struggled to control her tears. No wonder she hated being vulnerable. Life had taught her that only the strong survived.

"I've been trying to get a match with Vandenburg ever since Jimmy told me," Ray said. "Maybe this year."

Cooper nodded. "Yeah. We'll have to see what we can do about that."

Ray grinned. "Can't think of anything I'd like more than to make mincemeat of that prick."

Cooper could—*he'd* like to be the one to do it, with his bare fists.

It should have surprised him that he felt so fiercely about the wrongs that had been visited upon Jamie, but after last night he was over with being surprised where she was concerned.

She was under his skin in a big way. It was more than great sex. How much more, he had no idea. He was sailing into uncharted waters, big-time. And his gut told him that it would be rough going all the way. But when had anything ever been easy where Jamie was concerned?

"Thanks for coming to clear the air, Ray. I appreciate it," he said.

Cooper stared at his closed office door for a few minutes after the other man had left.

What was he going to do with Jamie Sawyer? Last night he'd committed to staying on as her trainer, yet this morning Ray's revelations and his reaction to them had shown him that he was far from objective where she was concerned. He couldn't bring himself to cut her loose, either, not when he knew how much she burned to redeem herself and her family. Who was he to deny her that chance?

And how was he going to work closely with her and not want her again, now that he knew how good it felt to be inside her?

Scrubbing his face with his hands, Cooper pushed himself to his feet. When in doubt, work out had always been his motto, and he headed out to hit the long bag and work up a sweat.

THAT AFTERNOON, Jamie exited her car in the parking lot at Fitzgerald Fighters' Gym. Her grandfather slammed his door shut on the other side of the car and fanned his face.

"Another stinker," he said, squinting up at the clear blue sky.

He'd insisted on coming into the gym with her when she'd told him that Cooper knew she was a Sawyer. He wanted to apologize in person for lying to Cooper. She wasn't about to stop him. She felt bad enough for asking him to lie in the first place. He'd never been comfortable with the subterfuge, even if he'd understood her reasons for wanting anonymity.

She jingled the car keys in her hand. Her palms were sweaty.

Her grandfather glanced her way.

"What's up?"

"Nothing."

She and Cooper had had sex last night. It was no big deal. It didn't change anything. In fact, it was supposed to make things better, release the tension.

Yeah, right.

She kept telling herself that the first five minutes would be the most uncomfortable, then maybe she'd make some crack or Cooper would be a smart-ass and all would return to normal. Whatever the hell that was.

She'd woken that morning to a rush of hot, sticky memories and a wave of… Not quite regret, but close. Sex with Cooper hadn't been what she'd expected. It had been great. It had also been disturbingly intense.

Now she had to face him for the first time.

This is why they invented that rule, don't screw the crew.

Funny how these things always seemed far more manageable when lust was raging and getting naked was on the agenda. Only in the cold light of day were all the pitfalls evident.

The first thing she saw when she walked into the gym was a sea of backs. Everyone—staff and fighters—were gathered around the ring. Alarm raced up her spine when she saw Cooper was in there, sparring with Ray. Both men were wearing boxing shorts and tank tops as well as padded head protectors and gloves.

In her one week in the gym, she had never seen Cooper spar with anyone, which was nothing less than what she'd expected—the man had suffered a badly detached retina. Any head trauma could aggravate it and lead to permanent blindness.

So what the hell was he doing trading punches with Ray? He might be wearing a head guard, but Cooper was still taking a stupid risk, and for what? To give Ray a workout? Or was this more about what he'd said the other day when they were running? About him not ever knowing anything other than fighting and missing it?

Dropping her bag, Jamie found a gap in the crowd and stood with her arms crossed over her chest.

She'd seen Ray fight live many times, but she'd only ever seen Cooper on the small screen. Even though she was deeply concerned about the risk he was taking, she couldn't help but admire the speed and grace of his footwork and the skill with which he ducked and weaved. Many heavyweight fighters were sluggers, shuffling around the ring and using power to pummel their opponents into submission. Cooper possessed a rare combination of grace and power, and Ray was having a hard time keeping up.

After a few minutes of trading blows, Cooper put his hand up and called an end to the bout. Both he and Ray were breathing heavily and laughing, the big lugs, as they pulled off their gloves.

"Man, you're fast," Ray said appreciatively. "Lucky you're retired, that's all I'm saying."

"Lucky you were going easy on me," Cooper said.

They climbed out of the ring together. Jamie glared at Cooper. How could he behave so cavalierly when his eyesight was at risk?

A couple of the other fighters were patting him on the back when he glanced across and saw her standing there. An absurd rush of warmth washed through her as she met his dark blue eyes and remembered the way he'd held her gaze as he slid inside her last night. Annoyed with herself, she shrugged it off.

"Can I see you for a moment?" she asked.

He nodded, grabbing a towel and following her as she marched through to his office. She waited until he was inside before kicking the door shut with her foot and turning to face him, arms crossed over her chest again.

"What were you doing, fighting Ray? What if he'd hit you in the head?"

Cooper's eyebrows rose. "Why do I feel as though I've been called into the principal's office?" he asked.

"I'm serious, Cooper. What if he'd clocked you a good one and you injured your eye again? For a stupid sparring match, for God's sake!"

Cooper stared at her for a beat, then his lips curved into a smile. "I didn't know you cared."

"I don't," she said quickly. "You were the one going on about not going blind the other day."

"Yet you're the one who just hauled me in here and tore strips off me," Cooper said, cocking his head to one side and studying her. "I think I'm flattered. After you kicked me out last night I figured I mustn't have been up to scratch."

Even though she knew he was deliberately provoking her, her cheeks grew warm.

"I didn't kick you out. It was just that my grandfather was due home. It wasn't a comment on your, um, performance."

"Oh. Good. That's a load off," he said. He was still grinning.

"Smart-ass."

"Sexy ass."

She stared at him, painfully aware of the urge to reach out and touch him. To slide her hand around one of his bulging biceps and snake her leg around one of his legs and press herself against the firmness of his body.

She sucked in a deep breath. Wasn't this stuff supposed to go away now that they'd had sex? Wasn't that the whole point of last night?

Cooper's smile faded as he stared back at her.

"Once was never going to be enough, was it?" she asked.

"No."

"Now what are we going to do?"

He shrugged. "Suck it up and get over it. We're both adults."

She knew it was the right answer, the best answer, the answer they should have stuck with all along. She still felt the sting of disappointment. That in itself was reason enough to agree with him. Sex was sex—it shouldn't come accessorized with feelings of longing and concern for Cooper's health and disappointment that whatever this was between them was over before it even began.

"Okay. But you're going to have to keep your shirt on around me," she said.

"And I never want to see those hot pants in my gym again. Deal?"

Despite how grim she felt right now, and how hard she knew it was going to be not thinking about Cooper's hot hands and hot mouth and hot cock, she found herself smiling. At least they were both in this thing together, strapping themselves to their respective masts to avoid the siren's song of their mutual attraction.

"Deal." They shook hands as a knock sounded on the door.

"Come in," Cooper said, releasing her hand.

"Just wanted to say my piece, if you've got a moment." It was her grandfather, looking determined.

"Of course," Cooper said.

Arthur's expression was unreadable as he approached, chin forward. "I wasn't comfortable lying to you, I want you to know that, and I'm sorry. It's not the way I usually like to handle things."

Jamie had to look away. Her grandfather had lost everything else already—his good name, his son, his standing in his chosen community. She hated knowing that she'd taken something else from him when she'd asked him to lie for her.

"You were standing by Jamie. I'm not saying I like being made a fool of, but I understand why you felt the need to do it. It's good to know Jamie's got people who will back her up. Every fighter needs a loyal team in their corner," Cooper said.

Jamie shot a look at his face, sure that she'd heard something else beneath his words.

"Well. Good. We understand each other," her grandfather said. He offered Cooper his hand and the two men shook.

There was a small awkward silence in the office afterward, the three of them standing there as though they were waiting for something else to happen. Cooper broke it by turning to Jamie, one eyebrow cocked in question.

"I'm pretty sure one of us is supposed to be out on the speedball right now, doing her conditioning training," he said.

Jamie forced a smile, even though she was feeling troubled after the events of the past few minutes. Troubled by what she'd forced her grandfather to do and because even though she knew keeping her relationship with Cooper professional was the smart thing to do, a part of her wanted him very, very badly. Last night, with his body moving inside hers and his heat warming her, she'd felt the best she had in a long time.

"Guess I'd better get my butt into gear, then," she said.

She was very aware of the two men watching her as she left

Cooper's office. One man was the most important person in her world—and she was a little disturbed to realize that Cooper was quickly moving into second place.

He's your trainer. He's supposed to be an important part of your life.

But like her grandfather, she'd never been a great liar, even when she was only lying to herself.

THREE HOURS LATER, Jamie walked out of the change room, her hair dripping water down her back from the shower.

Her grandfather had taken the bus home earlier. The heat always tired him out. She guessed he'd be napping by now with the curtains drawn and the fan on.

Across the gym, Cooper was working with one of the young fighters he'd taken on. Peter was a cocky bastard, but she could see why Cooper liked him. He was tough and determined, and with the right training and some luck he could go places.

She watched Cooper demonstrating a combination on the long bag. He made it look effortless, shifting his weight on his feet, his big arms bulging. It was a crying shame he'd had to retire.

Shouldering her bag, she turned for the door. Standing around watching Cooper was not a smart move. Not after the discussion they'd had in his office earlier.

Heat rose off the asphalt in shimmering waves as she made her way to her car. The door handle burned her fingers as she flipped it open. She dug her towel out of her bag to protect herself from the sting of the hot vinyl upholstery.

After she won her first decent purse and they'd moved apartments, she was getting a new car. Something made in this century. With air-conditioning.

Bracing herself for the stuffiness inside the car, she climbed behind the wheel and slid the key into the ignition. The engine churned for a second then made an ear-splitting metallic screech. Jamie jerked her hand away from the ignition.

She was no mechanic, but that sounded bad. Expensive bad.

She stared out the windshield for a long moment. If she juggled funds and maxed out her credit card, she could scrape together five hundred for repairs. Just. If it was any more than that, she was screwed.

"Shit."

She shoved the door open in a vain attempt at creating a cross breeze and pulled out her cell phone. The automotive association's helpline switched her over to a queue for service. She cranked the seat back a little. This was going to take some time.

After ten minutes, she got through to the call center, who promised a tow truck would be there, within two hours.

Great.

She shot a look toward the gym. It was cooler in there, and she could ask one of the guys on the counter to keep an eye on the parking lot for when the tow truck turned up.

She didn't move.

She told herself it was because she didn't want to risk missing the tow truck.

The truth was, she didn't want Cooper to know she was having car trouble. She knew he'd offer to help, and she didn't want to be cast in the role of damsel in distress. Maybe if they hadn't had sex, she wouldn't feel so strongly. But she did.

A little heat wouldn't kill her. She cranked the seat all the way back, propped her feet on the dash and closed her eyes. Man, it was hot. Sweat ran down her back, and the air felt heavy in her lungs.

She'd been waiting nearly forty minutes when she heard the crunch of gravel as someone approached.

She knew it was Cooper without looking.

"Car trouble?"

"Working on my tan."

She opened her eyes. He'd changed out of his gym gear, and

he wore dark sunglasses, a navy linen shirt and a pair of three-quarter khaki cargo pants and flip-flops. His hair was wet from the shower.

She closed her eyes again. He was too attractive. It was unfair, and she was only human.

"I'll give you a lift home," he said.

"I need my car for work tomorrow."

"Jamie, it's five o'clock. No mechanic in the world is going to fix it overnight."

She opened her eyes.

"A tow truck is on the way."

"Jason can take care of it for you."

"I can take care of it myself."

Cooper's lips moved as he said something with four letters under his breath.

"Fine. Have it your way," he said.

"I usually do."

He walked away. She spent the next ten minutes trying to think of anything other than the way he'd touched her last night. Sex had never been this complicated before.

A tap on the window made her start, and she glanced across to see Cooper standing on the passenger side of the car, a big vanilla ice-cream cone in hand. Frowning, she leaned across to unlock the door.

Cooper slid into the passenger seat.

"What are you doing?" she asked.

"Waiting with you."

"Why?"

He licked the ice cream. "What's wrong with the car?"

She rolled her eyes. Was he kidding?

"I think the fetzer valve needs replacing, and maybe it needs a new hornswoggle," she said.

He turned his head toward her. Even with his sunglasses on, she knew he was giving her a dry look.

"How the hell would I know?" she said. "I'm not a mechanic. I turned the key, it made a horrible noise. I called the automotive association. End of story."

"Sounds like the starter motor." He took another taste. "You want some ice cream?" He offered her the cone.

"It's not on my diet."

"Yeah. Sorry. Gotta say, it's one bonus about being retired."

She glanced away as he licked the ice cream again. No man's tongue should look that good.

"Is a starter motor expensive?" she asked.

"Depends. You could probably get a reconditioned one. They're cheaper."

She nodded, filing the information away.

"I suppose if I offer to lend you my car until yours is fixed, you'll say no," he asked.

"Depends. Are we talking about the Ferrari or the big black four-wheel-drive thing?"

"Which do you think?"

"Cool. I've always wanted to drive a Ferrari."

He'd reached the cone and it crunched loudly as he bit into it.

"I'm not lending you the Ferrari," he said.

"No shit."

He snorted a laugh. "It's an insurance thing, that's all."

"You keep telling yourself that."

He bit down on the last of the ice cream, then pushed his sunglasses on top of his head. He turned to face her, challenge in every line of his body.

"Okay, you can drive the Ferrari. I'll take you back to my place and you can pick it up right now."

Her lips curled into a reluctant smile. This man knew how to play hardball.

"It'd serve you right if I said yes."

He shook his head, a smile on his lips. "Do you ever accept help from anyone?"

Jamie flashed to the last time she'd put her well-being in another person's hands.

"Nope. How about you?"

He cranked his seat back and propped his feet on the sill of the open door.

"Did you hear Mayweather's taking on Mosley in New York?" He slid his sunglasses back over his eyes.

"Yeah. Mayweather's going to whip his ass," she said.

The smell of his aftershave was heavy in the air. It reminded her of last night. She wriggled in her seat.

"You don't have to wait with me," she said. "Really."

"I think Mosley's got a chance. Did you see that fight he had with Cotto last year? He's a nice fighter."

Jamie turned her head to look at him. He wasn't going anywhere. She wasn't accepting his offer to borrow one of his cars.

A standoff.

She liked Cooper Fitzgerald. A lot.

Probably it was just as well that they were never going to have sex again. Liking someone she had great sex with could only lead to trouble.

"I saw the fight. Mosely was good. But Mayweather is in better form. And Ray's better than both of them," she said loyally.

"True. But time will prove that," Cooper said confidently.

He waited with her until it started to get dark and the tow truck finally came. Nearly three hours, talking on and off, trading boxing anecdotes—her about her grandfather, him about his own career.

When she climbed up into the tow truck beside the driver, her car on the hoist behind them, Cooper gave her a stern look.

"If you need a lift tomorrow, call."

"I won't," she said.

"Yeah, I know."

He waited for the truck to pull onto the road before he turned back toward the gym. His shoulders looked big and broad silhouetted against the brightly lit facade.

"Can't believe I just met Cooper Fitzgerald," the driver said. "I saw that fight he had with Lennox Lewis. Man, he was good."

Jamie turned her eyes to the road.

"Yeah, he's the best."

And she was starting to realize that sleeping with him might have been the stupidest thing she'd ever done.

TWO WEEKS LATER, Cooper stood outside the gym's ring and watched Mick and Jamie go head-to-head in a sparring round. They'd been going at each other for nearly ten minutes. Mick had put the pressure on a number of times, but not once had Jamie made the mistake of thinking with her feet.

If anything, Mick was the one feeling the pressure as Jamie peppered him with body shots, using the combinations they'd been drilling for the past weeks. She was very good. He knew in his gut she was a real contender, and that she had the fire and the will to go all the way.

It was time to start talking to people about her next fight.

She was still a virtual unknown, with only two fights to her name, but he was confident he could get her something with a reasonable standing and a decent purse.

She needed the money. She'd been closemouthed about how much it had cost to repair her car, and he'd seen the apartment she shared with her grandfather. She worked long hours, taking on extra shifts when she could, yet she still trained harder than half his guys. A decent purse would make a big difference in her life.

He could still remember the change each fight had made to his world as he'd won his way up the rankings. Decent food, decent clothes, the ability to stop mooching off Harry and his wife and find a place of his own. Soon Jamie would have a chance to experience the same sense of achievement.

The sooner he went into his office and started making calls the sooner she'd be on her way to the top.

A few of the guys watching gave hoots of approval as Jamie landed a good jab straight into Mick's chin.

Cooper frowned and forced himself to face something he'd been avoiding for a few weeks now. He didn't want to put Jamie in the ring to face another professional bout.

He didn't want her to get hurt. Which was why it had been a really stupid idea to sleep with her, because now every time he looked at her he saw a woman first and a fighter second. That was something they could get away with in training, but once she was standing in the ring facing someone who wanted to break her, it was going to be a problem.

He was going to be a problem. He didn't want to watch her get bruised and battered. He wanted to protect her. Make her laugh. Take her to bed.

Last week he'd booked a fight for Ray—a big purse, with a hard-ass contender from the States. Ray would have to put on his A-game and even then be extra sharp if he was to win. But not once had Cooper second-guessed himself or feared for his fighter or wanted to talk Ray out of the bout.

Whereas he couldn't even think about booking Jamie a fight without feeling as if he wanted to punch something.

He closed his eyes. He really was an idiot. Of all the women he'd encountered over all his years of living, why was Jamie Sawyer the only one who'd ever inspired these emotions in him? She was stubborn, proud, driven, defensive. She took on every day as though it was a battle, and she viewed everyone, except her grandfather, with prickly suspicion.

Cooper admired her. He understood the urge to fight and keep fighting, no matter what. It was what had driven him to climb out his bedroom window when he was twelve years old, aching and bruised from the most recent beating courtesy of his mother's latest boyfriend. He'd decided then and there that life on his own could not be more dangerous and painful than life under his unreliable, drug-addicted mother's roof. He'd been both right and wrong. Like Jamie, he'd had to learn how to look after himself. How to toughen up. How to protect himself. How to hit first to avoid being a victim.

His mother was dead now. She'd overdosed when he was twenty. He'd made sure she had a decent burial, even if he hadn't attended the service himself. He'd figured he'd owed her that much and no more. Back then, his life had been all about what was owed, not what was given or offered freely. Over the years he'd unlearned some of those tough lessons that the street had taught him. Harry's generosity, Cooper's own growing maturity, the comfort and safety of success—all of those elements had combined to bring him to a point in his life where he'd looked at Jamie Sawyer being beaten around the ring and been unable to stand back and let it happen when he had the power to make a difference.

Now she was in his life, and every day he saw more of the woman she could be if she didn't have such a ferocious fire burning in her belly. He liked that woman a lot, almost as much as he admired the warrior in her. Almost as much as he desired her strong, sexy body.

Cooper swore under his breath and retreated to his office. For a long moment he sat staring at his desktop, his head in his hands.

Then he dragged the phone toward himself and flicked open his address book. For an hour he made the rounds, talking to his connections, building up Jamie, putting out the feelers to see what was out there, what was possible. When he'd finished, he dropped the phone and pushed himself away from the desk.

Now they waited. It might take a while to hear back, maybe a day or two. Jamie would keep training, and he would keep telling himself that not only did she need a trainer more than a lover, but also she didn't want the latter at all.

He was on his way out to the gym when the phone rang. He turned back to answer it.

After a brief exchange of words, he started to write down dates and figures.

"I'll need to get back to you on a few details," he said.

Brian Hoyland was a small-time promoter and one of the first calls he'd made.

"Sure. Get back to me. It's a good offer."

"It's damned fast, that's for sure."

"I had a cancellation, you know how it is," Brian said.

Cooper ended the call and rubbed the bridge of his nose. He hadn't expected things to move this quickly. Hadn't wanted them to.

He left the office. Jamie was doing stretches on one of the mats, her body glowing with a fine sheen of perspiration.

She looked up at him as he approached.

"Before you ask, I've done all my sit-ups," she said.

"You've been offered a fight."

Her face lit with anticipation. "Really? That's great."

No, it's not. You're going to get hurt. And I am beginning to realize that you are the last person in the world I want to see hurt.

"Yeah."

He was her trainer. He would train her. Do his job.

Not matter how hard that was shaping up to be.

7

THREE WEEKS LATER, Cooper stepped out of the shower cubicle in his motel room and reached for the towel. Thin and scratchy, like the motel itself, it had seen better days. But it was clean, as were his sheets and the bathroom.

It wasn't as if they'd had a world of choice in a rural town the size of Dubbo. Situated about five hours' drive west of Sydney, it was a city of forty thousand souls and no five-star hotels. It was also the city where Jamie would be taking on her next opponent, a Melbourne fighter named Liana Nelson.

The fight was tomorrow night, the venue the city's biggest sporting auditorium. Jamie and Liana were the first fight on the bill, with a number of male boxers rounding out the night.

Liana was huge, taller than Jamie, built. She was pushing the weight limit for the middleweight class and he'd heard that she'd barely squeaked by at this afternoon's weigh-in. She was an experienced fighter, with fifteen wins to her name and only one loss. Like Jamie, it had come early in her career. She'd made a habit of winning ever since.

Cooper was still a little surprised that the other woman had been willing to take on a newcomer like Jamie. It wasn't as though Liana needed wins. She was at the stage in her career where she was looking for title shots, not runs on the board. But no matter what her motivation, it was a good fight for Jamie.

They'd only been able to source a grainy amateur tape of Liana's most recent bout in the weeks since the fight had been scheduled. It had shown a ferocious fighter who came out hard and aimed to put her opponents away as early as possible. Cooper and Jamie had studied it over and over, noting Liana's habits, talking about her weak spots.

There weren't many. She sometimes dropped her guard hand before lashing out with her killer uppercut. And she tended to come out fighting when she got hurt, thrashing around with little skill or strategy. If Jamie could antagonize her, they could use that temper against her. But Jamie had to withstand the other woman's onslaught first.

He sat on the edge of the bed and ran both hands through his hair. This was a lot harder than he'd imagined it would be.

In nearly eighteen years of competitive boxing, he'd never felt this nervous before a fight. It had taken every bit of self control he possessed to stop himself from conveying his fears to Jamie when they did a light training session this afternoon. She'd been quiet and inwardly focused. He hadn't tried to draw her out. The last thing she needed was the knowledge of just how distracted and screwed-up her trainer was.

He let his towel drop and crossed to his suitcase to find underwear. A knock at the door had him reaching for the towel again. He held it securely in one fist at his hip as he opened the door.

Jamie stood there, her face pale.

"I need to talk," she said.

Her eyes slid down his body. His heart kicked into gear, slamming against his ribs. One look—he was so hooked on her it wasn't funny.

"Give me a moment," he said, shutting the door.

Jamie and near nudity were not a good mix. Already he was half-hard simply because she'd been within arm's reach. By the time this was all over, he figured he'd have definitely earned himself that sainthood.

He dressed quickly in jeans and a T-shirt then let her in.

"Okay, what's up?" he asked as she brushed past him and sank onto one of the twin beds.

"I can't stop thinking about that uppercut. What if I don't see it coming? I'm worried I won't be able to take it," Jamie said. She rested her elbows on her knees, leaning forward. Her face was tight with worry.

"Yep, and you won't know if you can or not until it lands." He sat opposite her. She scowled.

"Thanks for the words of reassurance."

"It's the truth. There's a bunch of stuff she might throw at you in the ring that you might not be able to take. You won't know until you're there and that leather hits you and hurts you. Nothing I say is going make any difference to that. *Nothing.*"

He held her eye. She let out a big gust of air.

"Okay. Okay," she said, flopping back onto the bed.

She was wearing a pair of hip-hugging, skin-tight jeans. Because he wasn't a saint just yet, his gaze traveled up her long, lithe legs before tracing up her belly and over her breasts. She was focused on the ceiling, and he decided it was good that she couldn't see the way he was looking at her, remembering what it had been like to be inside her, remembering all the times he'd fantasized about being with her again over the past few months. She'd ruined him for any other woman and lately he'd been reduced to the teenage remedy of his own hand on too many occasions to count.

"Was Ray like this before his fight last week?" she asked.

They'd both gone to watch Ray fight. Even from Ray's corner he'd heard Jamie hollering her support from the front row. Ray's hard-fought win on points had been the first big-ticket coup of Cooper's training career—but it would be nothing compared to Jamie winning tomorrow night. Winning in the first round, on the first punch, before the other fighter even had a chance to breathe near her. That would be his absolute ideal.

Fat chance.

"Ray knew what he had to do. So do you," Cooper said. At least he could sound like a trainer even if he didn't feel like one.

"I just want to stop thinking. I was tired after the drive here and our training session, and I thought I could sack out early, get a good night's sleep.... Hell, Grandpa is out like a light. Fell asleep watching some cable news show. But my brain won't let up on me," Jamie said, eyes still on the ceiling.

Half the battle in the ring was psychological. A night spent second-guessing herself was not going to leave Jamie fresh and ready to fight tomorrow. She needed to be rested and alert.

Whenever he'd gotten like this before a fight, his trainer had called in a massage therapist to work the kinks out of his muscles. Hardly an option in the middle of rural Australia.

"Let's go for a walk," he said. It was late and they were on a highway with nothing much in the way of scenery in either direction, but at least it would be a distraction.

"Tried that," she said. "Didn't work."

Sitting up, she rotated her neck.

"Maybe I'll try another shower, or some hot milk. I guess my brain has to stop sometime, right?"

Or it could keep circling for hours, exhausting her and leaving her full of doubt.

Against his better judgment, he gestured toward the bed.

"Lie down. I'll give you a shoulder rub."

She stilled and gave him a look.

"I don't know whether that's really going to relax me a whole hell of a lot," she said. Her gaze ran up and down his body again.

"Then we go for a walk." He shrugged.

She hesitated, thinking over the two options. Then she slid backward on the bed and arranged herself facedown, toeing off her flip-flop sandals.

"Pretend I'm someone else," he said.

"Fine. Don't talk, don't breathe and go scrub off your after-shave and I'll have a fighting chance," she said.

He smiled tightly. It was like that for him, too. The huskiness of her voice. The way she laughed. The scent of her body. There were a million things about her that drove him wild. If she'd been moments away from straddling his back and laying hands on him, he knew he'd be hard as a rock and drilling a hole in the bed.

He frowned, one knee on the mattress. Given all of the above, what the hell was he doing, offering her a massage in the first place?

"Stringing it out isn't helping, by the way," she said.

Screw it. It was a back rub at the end of the day. He'd survived nearly five weeks of watching her move, laughing with her, running with her, spotting her while she trained.

There had been moments of intense temptation every day—the time when it had been only the two of them in the gym late at night, and he'd known she was naked in the shower in the women's change room and that he could go in there and have her against the lockers in seconds. The time when they'd been watching fight tape in his office early one morning and the scent of her newly washed hair had kept him on edge all day. The time when he'd driven her home after training and they'd sat tensely outside her apartment building for a long, long time, neither of them saying a word, before she finally got out of the car and went inside.

He could handle a back rub.

Straddling her hips, he leaned forward and placed his hands on her shoulders. Digging his thumbs in, he started to work. She let out a groan of appreciation.

"Oh, that's good," she said.

That quickly, he was hard. Gritting his teeth, he concentrated on working on each of her muscle groups, mentally naming each body part as he worked his way down her back—the long flat planes of her trapezius and latissimus dorsi muscles, the rounded deltoid muscles on her shoulders, the long serratus muscles along her spine.

If only she didn't feel so warm and firm and alive beneath him, it might have worked. As it was, he was sweating and tense by the time he was rubbing the muscles around the small of her back.

"Okay. This is *so* not working," she said suddenly, her head snapping up. "It's been five weeks, Cooper. Five long, lonely weeks. I've been thinking about you touching me every day. And this is not how I imagined you doing it."

His hands stilled. He stared at the dark curtain of hair spilling over her shoulders and across the bed. His hard-on throbbed as he allowed himself to imagine how good it would be to roll her over, strip off her jeans and bury himself inside her again.

Good. Damned good.

But she had a fight tomorrow. A tough fight, from what they'd seen of her opponent. Jamie was relying on him to help her prepare for it, mentally and physically.

He couldn't sleep with her.

But maybe he could offer *her* something.

Relaxation. Release. Satisfaction.

"Roll over," he said. Before he could think twice.

Not that he was doing a hell of a lot of thinking with his upstairs brain right now. About five seconds after he'd flashed to an image of Jamie spread wild and wanton before him, his rational brain had gone off-line.

He'd been holding out for five weeks. And he wasn't a saint. Not even close.

JAMIE FROZE AS SHE heard Cooper's low, intense words. Then a rush of molten heat raced through her. She was already enormously turned on from having his hands on her for the past twenty minutes. Even through her T-shirt, Cooper's touch was incredible. Then there were the past five weeks of foreplay that they'd both endured.

Seeing him every day. Looking into his deep blue eyes.

Watching his white, straight teeth flash into a smile or a laugh. Trying not to stare when he worked on the long bag or did push-ups or sit-ups. It had been torture, pure torture. And now he was offering to end it. At least, she hoped he was.

Tomorrow night's fight floated to the top of her mind as she wriggled around until she was on her back, his big thighs straddling her thighs. She should stay focused, keep her relationship with Cooper pure and professional. She knew that it was the rational, sensible, right thing to do. But she wanted him so badly. She *ached* for him—a wet, hot ache that had been driving her crazy every night. No matter what she did, how she touched herself, it wasn't a substitute for him.

Maybe if she had him again, some of this needy, insane lust would ease. At the very least it would stop her from thinking about the fight, about Liana Nelson's big, square shoulders and fast hands.

"Just relax," Cooper said, reaching for the stud on her jeans.

She sucked in her breath as she felt his touch against her belly. His fingers found the tab on her fly and he slid it down purposefully. Her eyelids dropped to half-mast as he peeled her jeans off. She lifted her hips to help him as he tugged the denim down and over her ankles. His hot blue gaze devoured her, gliding up her legs, seeking the juncture between her thighs, making her even hotter than she already was.

She could still remember how big he'd been, how he'd stretched her, how complete and satisfied she'd felt when he was inside her.

She smiled as she anticipated experiencing all that again.

He hooked his fingers into the waistband of her black satin panties and pulled them off. This time when he looked at her, she could see the naked hunger in his face.

"Spread your legs," he ordered, his hands resting on her knees.

She did so willingly, her heart pounding hard. His expression was intent as he mapped her with his eyes. She kept her curls waxed into a neat strip on her mound, but she liked it bare between her legs. She could tell by the way his fingers tightened around her knees that he was enjoying the view.

"I've been wondering for a long time what you'd taste like," he said.

Moving down the bed, he settled himself. His breath was warm against her inner thighs. All her muscles tightened as he lowered his head toward her.

Oh boy.

She closed her eyes and let her head drop back as he traced a wet, delicate path along the seam of her sex, working his way up toward her mound. Reaching his goal, he repeated the action again and again, each time exerting a little more pressure, delving a little more deeply between her folds until at last he'd penetrated all her secrets and had teased out the already hard nub of her clitoris. She shuddered and spread her thighs wider as he began to taste her in earnest, his tongue circling, flicking, pressing flat against her, rasping against her sensitive flesh.

Need pooled in her belly and she circled her hips as he began to use his hands, one to spread her wide so he could devour her with openmouthed kisses, the other to begin teasing at her inner lips, a single finger slicking around and around her entrance but never quite penetrating.

She was on fire. She pushed her fingers into his hair and rode the crest of a wave of desire, her body trembling.

At last he slid a finger inside her, then another. Her hands fisted in his hair as he sucked her clitoris into his mouth and flicked it over and over again with his tongue, his fingers moving in and out of her all the while.

She gasped. The tension in her ratcheted tighter and tighter. He slid a third finger inside her and she came, a wordless cry flying from her lips. Her body shuddered. Her back arched.

He eased her gently back down to earth, kissing her mound,

soothing her with his fingers, pressing kisses against the tender skin of her thighs. She watched lazily as, at last, he shifted away from her. His eyes were heavy-lidded with desire. She waited for him to undress and rejoin her.

But he didn't start to strip. Instead, he sat on the edge of the bed. She only understood that it was all over when he stood and collected her discarded jeans and underwear.

She propped herself up on her elbows and stared at him as he dropped her clothes beside her.

"You are not doing this to me again," she said. "No way."

"You're fighting tomorrow," he said.

As though that explained everything.

"Having sex is not going to stop me from fighting," she said.

He ran a hand over the back of his neck.

"I don't want you to get hurt, Jamie. It's bad enough as it is, and tonight will only make it harder."

His voice was quiet, low. For a moment she didn't understand what he meant.

"I already told you, I don't do love, Cooper," she said. "You don't have to worry about me getting clingy or taking things the wrong way."

"Jesus, I *wish* that was what I'm worried about," he said. "I meant I don't want to watch you take hits tomorrow night."

She blinked. Then the full import of what he'd said and what it meant sunk in.

Cooper had feelings for her. Feelings that went beyond wanting to have sex with her.

She reached for her underwear. The lazy languor of a few minutes ago was gone, big-time.

"I can't control how you feel," she said as she slid her legs into her jeans.

"I don't recall saying you could."

"You feeling responsible for me is not part of our deal. I need a trainer, not a protector."

"This isn't something I saw coming, either," he said.

"I don't need you to look after me. I don't want you to. All I need is for you to help me train and get fights."

"Aren't you forgetting something? You want me to have sex with you, too, when you want it, how you want it," he said, his jaw set.

"You wanted it as much as I did," she said. "Don't pretend you weren't hard for me every time. You could have walked away."

"I should have," he said. "I had no business sleeping with one of my fighters."

She stared at him. Something caught in her belly at the haunted look in his eyes and the tense set to his shoulders.

"It doesn't mean anything. It's just sex," she said.

He eyed her silently. She had to look away.

"I need to get some sleep," she said, heading for the door.

He didn't say another word. She waited until she'd closed the door behind her and walked around the corner before stopping and leaning against the cool brick wall.

There was a time in her life when having a man like Cooper Fitzgerald confessing he had feelings for her would have made her heart sing.

Those days were over.

It didn't matter if there had been just a moment there when he'd said those words and a part of her had unfolded, warm and welcoming and hopeful.

Swearing at her own stupidity, Jamie pushed away from the wall. *Warm* and *welcoming?* How about gooey and weak and pathetic? How about soft and willing and perfect victim material?

What's it going to take for you to learn? What else do you need to lose before you smarten up?

Her back straight, Jamie made her way to her room.

Cooper would get over it. He'd have to, because he wasn't ever going to get what he wanted from her.

COOPER WAS DAMNED tempted to punch a hole in the wall when Jamie walked out the door.

There was something broken in her. Maybe it was the same thing that had once been broken in him, but he trusted himself and life enough now to take a risk. Jamie did not. Or could not. Same thing.

He'd seen her eyes go blank when she'd registered what he was saying. His feelings for her were about as welcome as a dose of the clap. Hell, she'd probably *prefer* the clap to his reluctant, ham-fisted declaration; at least she could treat that with a couple of doses of antibiotics. Him, she'd have to face day after day.

Shit.

Even though he'd never been the kind of man who drowned his sorrows, he poured himself an overpriced glass of bourbon from the minibar. Sitting on the bed, he tossed back a mouthful and hissed at the burn.

He nursed the glass in his hand and tried not to remember the sweet sounds of Jamie's desire. Out of the corner of his eye, he could see the bed, rumpled from her passion. She'd been so hot, so turned on. It had nearly driven him over the edge. Never had he got off on a woman's pleasure so much. Every sound she made, every hitch in her breathing, every twitch of her hips, the way her hands had clutched at his hair. Without a doubt, one of the most intense sexual experiences of his life, and he'd been fully clothed the whole time.

He raised the bourbon to his mouth, then stared down at the golden liquid. He stood and poured it down the sink in the bathroom. Was there anything more tragic than a lonely, horny ex-boxer sitting in a shitty motel room tossing back room-service bourbon? He couldn't think of a single thing.

Grabbing his room key, he strode out into the night. Two miles up the darkened highway, and two miles back. Hands jammed into his pockets, his thoughts circular.

Was he falling in love with Jamie? Was that what all this

bullshit was about? He had no measuring stick, no benchmark to go by since he'd never loved a woman before. Never trusted it, never wanted it, never pursued it. In the back of his mind, there'd always been too many dark shadows from the past. Images of his mom being slapped around, or passed out on the couch, a needle lying beside her on the carpet. Domestic harmony hadn't exactly been the catch cry of his childhood.

He'd avoided love. Until now. Then Jamie had skyrocketed into his life, undeniable from the very beginning.

Which left him where, exactly? He snorted an unamused laugh as he saw the lights of the motel looming ahead.

Who was he kidding? He was nowhere, with a fistful of nothing, with no expectation of anything changing.

Not once had Jamie given any indication that she saw him as anything more than a handy hard body to get off on. And no, the undeniable chemistry and passion between them meant jack. Especially when her first reaction to the news that he cared for her was to hightail it out of his room as though he'd pulled a gun on her.

To top it all off, he had to watch her fight tomorrow.

Fan-freakin'-tastic.

He finally fell asleep at around one in the morning. He woke feeling gritty-eyed and short-tempered. Jamie was out by the pool, lying in the sun with a boxing magazine. He spared one glance at her super-fit body in a black bikini before walking in the opposite direction.

On the day of a fight, a boxer's only responsibility was to stay loose and to chow down on carbs before the match. Arthur had already located a pasta restaurant in town and Cooper knew that the Sawyers planned to be there at midday for Jamie to load up. They didn't need him to watch her eat. He stayed away from her 'til late afternoon when he spotted her once again out by the pool, this time sitting in a yoga pose, doing some kind of meditation.

He made plenty of noise so she knew he was approaching. Her ponytail swished over her shoulder as she glanced at him.

"How are you feeling? Rested?" he asked.

"Yep. Had a good lunch, plenty of fluids," she said.

"Okay. Your bout's at seven. I figure we should get over there about five or so," Cooper said, shoving his hands into his pockets.

She nodded and stood in one fluid, graceful movement. "I'll go grab a shower."

He turned to leave.

"Cooper," she said.

He glanced back at her, and she held his eye. "If the fight goes hard, if she hurts me, I don't want you throwing in the towel," she said.

He jerked his head as though she'd taken a shot at him.

"Excuse me?"

"You heard me. If it gets ugly, I don't want you trying to protect me," she said. "I need a chance to win this fight."

"And you think I'm going to take that chance away from you?" he asked.

He was a boxer. He knew the work she'd put in, how hungry she was for this. He'd never do that to her, no matter how much it killed him to see her in pain.

She shrugged. "I don't know. I figured, in light of what happened last night, that I should lay it on the table."

He rounded on her and moved in close. She held her ground where a lot of men wouldn't have.

"I will do my job. If you're hurt and you can't fight, I *will* give up the fight. Do not have any doubt about that, okay? And there is nothing you can say that will change that, Jamie. Equally, if you're just getting an old-fashioned pounding, I won't take away your chance. After all, I know how much all this means to you."

Her chin came up. "It does. It means everything," she said.

"Exactly," he said.

He walked away from her. He didn't trust himself to say

anything further. She needed to get her head on straight for the fight. Maybe he should have bitten his tongue altogether, but there was no way he could have let that comment stand. Did she honestly think he was going to hand the fight over to Liana Nelson because of what he'd said about not wanting to watch her get hurt?

He fought the urge to turn on his heel and go back and list for her all the shit he'd had to endure in his life, all the moments that had made it possible for him to stand by tonight and watch her have pain inflicted on her, even though it would test his will to the nth degree.

He kept walking until he was in his room. For the next ten minutes, he concentrated on putting his kit together. Towels, water, Jamie's mouth guard, gauze tape for her hands, coach's tape for the laces on her gloves and boots, Vaseline for her face, an ice pack and, finally, the No-Swell, a piece of metal that he would keep in a bucket of ice beside the ring and press on her cheekbones, brow and jaw between rounds to reduce swelling.

Jamie was waiting beside the car with her grandfather when Cooper emerged with his kit and a bucket in hand. She was dressed in a warm-up suit and her hair was braided tight to her skull. The look she gave him was challenging. He sent it straight back at her.

They drove the ten minutes to the auditorium in silence. There were a lot of media vans in the parking lot. Cooper frowned as he parked in a slot near the front entrance. He turned to Arthur.

"Any of the guys fighting tonight have a profile I don't know about?" he asked.

Arthur shrugged and looked equally bemused.

Then they walked through the double doors into the foyer, and reporters swarmed them from every direction, snapping into action like well-trained soldiers the moment they caught sight of their prey.

"Ms. Sawyer, can you comment on why you've started your boxing career using a pseudonym? Are you trying to fool the boxing public or are you ashamed of your father's history?"

"Ms. Sawyer, is it true you couldn't find anyone to train you and that Cooper Fitzgerald only took you on as a favor to a friend?"

"Ms. Sawyer, what do you say to the comment that you're simply cashing in on your name to try and score cheap points in the boxing ring?"

Flashes popped, reporters jostled forward and Jamie stood rooted to the spot, her face pale, her eyes wide with panic. Beside her, Arthur was red in the face. He pushed belligerently at the most aggressive of the reporters, yelling at them to back off. Cooper glanced around, spotting a pair of security guards heading their way.

"Hey. You want to do something about this?" he demanded. Then he turned on the reporters. "Ms. Sawyer has nothing to say. As you will see from tonight's fight, actions speak louder than words."

He forced his way between Jamie and the pack. Angling his body, he slid an arm around her shoulders and urged her toward the nearest door.

They emerged into the vast, empty silence of the auditorium. The moment they were through the door, Cooper let Jamie go and shot the bolt to prevent any reporters following them.

"What the frig was that?" Arthur demanded, his face a dangerous shade of red.

Remembering the old man's heart attack, Cooper grabbed a nearby folding chair and shoved it toward him.

"Sit," he ordered before turning to a pale-faced Jamie.

"How? No one knows, except for Ray and you and my grandfather," she said. Her voice quavered with uncertainty.

Damn it, he should have been more cautious. He should have at least gone inside on his own to check out the situation. That way Jamie would have had the chance to prepare herself. As it was, she'd been a sitting duck.

"I don't know. It doesn't matter. None of it matters except for what goes on between you and Liana Nelson in that ring tonight," he said. He had to refocus her and move her past the shock.

"Those questions. Did you hear what they were asking? My God," she said. Her hands were shaking as she worried at the handle of her sports bag.

He'd dealt with the media for a long time, and he figured she'd had her fair share of dealings with them after her father's fraud charges and his death. As far as Cooper was concerned, there was no such thing as journalistic ethics. It was all about headlines and selling newspapers. None of them gave a damn about who they stomped on along the way.

"Forget 'em," he said. "They're a pack of assholes, and they have no idea about you or your family. What they think or say is not important."

"Except for the fact that they print it in a newspaper that just happens to go out to hundreds of thousands of people," Jamie said.

Arthur swore, and Cooper spared a glance for the old man. His color was better, but he still looked agitated.

This was a huge psychological blow for Jamie, one that none of them had been prepared for.

"Let's go find your change room," he said.

She needed time to recover and process what had happened. He hoped a couple of hours was going to do it, because pretty soon she was going to be standing opposite a seasoned fighter who wanted nothing more than to wipe the canvas with Jamie's face.

They walked toward the glowing exit sign on the farthest side of the auditorium. Cooper moved forward to open the door, but it swung toward him before he could grasp the handle and he was forced to take a step back. A tall figure filled the doorway.

Cooper heard Jamie make a small, surprised noise behind him.

Kyle Vandenburg smiled, his dark gaze zeroing in on Jamie. In contrast to her, he didn't look even remotely surprised.

"Jimmy. It's good to see you," Vandenburg said.

Jamie's face might have been carved from stone. "What are you doing here?"

"I'm here with my girl, Liana," he said. He angled his body so they could see the woman waiting impatiently behind him in the corridor.

Liana Nelson's pale green eyes were belligerent as she surveyed them, a sneer on her lips.

Cooper had seen his fair share of psych-outs in his time, but this had to take the cake. Vandenburg had tipped off the media. Somehow, he must have gotten wind of Jamie's fledgling career and decided to exploit her for all it was worth. The quick fight offer, Liana's willingness to take on a virtual unknown—all of it made sense now. Jamie Holloway was no feather in Liana Nelson's cap—but Jamie *Sawyer* was a whole other matter. Liana could milk the publicity on this bout for months, maybe even parlay it into a title shot.

"Looking forward to seeing you square up, Jimmy," Vandenburg said. "Should be a good match."

Cooper stepped forward. He'd never liked Vandenburg, and he liked him even less since finding out what he'd done to Jamie. Watching him stand there as though he and Jamie were still on speaking terms, as though he hadn't set all this up to exploit her, made his blood boil.

"How about backing off?" Cooper said. "Before I make you."

Vandenburg flicked his dark gaze Cooper's way.

"Fitzgerald. I heard you'd been forced to retire. Bad luck, dude."

"It won't work," Cooper said. "You think this is going to give your girl the edge? Jamie's going to waste her, no matter what you try and throw at her. But then you never understood that fighting was all about heart, did you?"

Vandenburg's eyes flashed and Liana shot him a look as though she was asking for permission to do something more than stand by. Cooper took another step forward, forcing Vandenburg to hold his ground and confront Cooper or back up into the corridor.

He chose the latter. Cooper waited until Jamie and Arthur had slipped past him and were heading for the change rooms before he relinquished his possession of the doorway.

Without a word or a backward glance, he followed Jamie. The first thing he saw when he walked into the change room was Jamie sitting on a bench, her head in her hands. Slowly she lifted her ashen face.

"I don't think I can do this," she said.

8

JAMIE CLOSED HER EYES and hunched lower on the bench.

She'd been so psyched for this fight. So ready to go out there and win. Even the words she'd had with Cooper before they'd left the motel hadn't deterred her. If anything, they'd only reminded her of what she was fighting for.

Then she'd walked in the door of the auditorium and been bombarded by all those reporters. And Kyle...

She'd never wanted to see him again. Once she'd loved and trusted him totally, and he'd taken what he wanted and left her with nothing.

"So you're just going to let Vandenburg scare you off, are you?" Cooper asked.

Her head shot up.

"Don't try that amateur psychology crap on me, Cooper."

He spread his hands wide. "I'm not trying anything. It's the truth. Vandenburg purposely got this fight with you so he could pull all this off. Ambush you with the media, then rattle you by revealing himself. He wants to cash in on your name to win publicity for his girl, and he's banking on you being so thrown by this circus he's created that you'll lose the fight. Or, even better, that you'll pull out at the last minute, which will bring them even more publicity."

He was right. But it didn't stop the churning in her gut or the thoughts racing around her head.

"I just… I wasn't ready for this," she said. She hated that she sounded so shaken and small.

"Maybe we should pull out of the fight," Arthur said. "I don't like playing into that A-hole's hands, but if you're not up to this, Jimmy…"

Her grandfather's face was pinched with concern. She had a sudden flash of how he'd looked during those scary, terrifying days in the hospital. How pale and fragile and infinitely precious to her.

"She's up to it. Jamie's one of the toughest people I know," Cooper said.

He squatted in front of her, bringing his face to her level. He held her eye, his regard steady.

"Here's what you're going to do. You're going to go out and win that fight. Wipe the sneer off that steroid-junkie's face. And you're going to start doing what you set out to do—reclaiming your name."

Staring into his eyes, she could almost see herself doing it, exactly as he'd described.

"It's Jimmy's decision," her grandfather said. "If she's not happy, I'm not happy."

Cooper didn't take his eyes off her face. She couldn't look away from him.

She would hate herself if she backed out of this fight. She would feel like a victim again, the way she had when she'd discovered what Kyle and his business manager had done to her and her family.

But to have all those reporters watching, waiting for her to slip up. She'd always known this was coming. She'd imagined the moment of revelation a hundred times—but on her terms, not theirs.

"It doesn't matter," Cooper said as though he could read her mind. "You'll never be able to control the press. Ignore them. This is a fight, nothing more, nothing less. You and Liana Nelson in that ring. Ten rounds, one winner. Sweat and blood and leather."

She closed her eyes, struggling to do as he said and push everything else to one side. He was right, it didn't matter. At the end of the day, tonight was about her and Liana Nelson. About which one of them was stronger, both physically and psychologically.

"Come on, warrior woman," Cooper said, his voice so low she almost didn't catch what he'd said.

She lifted her gaze from the floor and met his eyes again. Then she gave a short, sharp nod. His lips curled into a small, approving smile. He braced his hands against his thighs and pushed himself to his feet.

"Let's get you taped and warmed up," he said.

Taking a deep breath, Jamie let it go on a sigh, consciously letting all the stress of the past half hour slide away with it. She'd come here to fight, and that was what she was going to do.

For the next hour, she warmed up. Skipping, shadow boxing, sit-ups, working with the focus mitts. Cooper talked to her quietly the entire time about Liana's weaknesses, the areas where Jamie could attack, things to look out for. When she was warm and loose, she stripped down to her underwear and Cooper gave her a brisk rubdown on the massage table the organizers had provided. For the first time, his touch did not set her world on fire. His hands were firm, warm, strong, but his touch was impersonal. Her mind was focused only on the battle to come. There was no room for anything else.

As he worked her muscles, Cooper reminded her of all the training they'd put in. All the hours of sweat and effort. He told her she was strong and fast and accurate. He reminded her of the sparring sessions she'd won against Mick in the gym, of her endurance and her power. The world shrank until there was just the deep reassurance of his voice and the feel of his hands on her body.

Her body shiny with oil, she dressed in her fight trunks and sports crop, ensuring her chest guard was fitted properly. She put her boots on, then watched Cooper tape the laces down so that they didn't come undone during the fight. Finally she sat on the edge of the table and waited as Cooper wrapped her hands.

"How does that feel?" he asked.

She flexed both hands into fists. "Good."

Cooper slid her gloves on and secured the laces, taping them down. Holding her chin in one hand, he rubbed Vaseline across her face, concentrating on her brow and cheekbones. They were so close she could see the individual whiskers of his stubble and feel his breath on her face each time he exhaled. She could see how long and dark his eyelashes were and trace the bump on his nose. She remembered the story he'd told her that night when they waited for her car to be towed, about the first time he'd had it broken in the ring.

The silence stretched. She closed her eyes to avoid looking at him.

"It'd be ironic if this stuff turned out to be great for my complexion, huh?" she said.

Anything to dispel the growing sense of intimacy. She had enough crap whirling around in her head without adding more confusion to the mix.

"Even if it was, I think it's safe to say that getting smacked in the face a few dozen times is going to cancel that out," Cooper said.

"Yeah, well, there's always that," she said.

When she opened her eyes again, he was watching her intently.

"Keep your guard up, okay? I don't ever want to see that hand dropping. You protect yourself every second," he said.

Something flashed deep in his eyes, something protective and fierce. She looked away.

His hand landed on her back, heavy and warm.

"You're a fighter, Jamie. Take it up to her, make her angry, then lay her out."

She nodded, then slid off the massage table. Her grandfather had watched from a chair against the wall throughout, but he stood now and made two fists with his hands.

"You go get 'em, Spitfire," he said, tapping his fists against her gloves.

She laughed. "Spitfire?"

"Every boxer needs a name," her grandfather said. "Jamie Spitfire Sawyer sounds pretty good to me."

A knock sounded on the door. The referee entered, neat in his black pants, white shirt and bow tie.

For the next five minutes, he explained the rules of the bout to Jamie, all standard. Before he exited, he warned that they were only minutes away from fight time.

"Let's go," Cooper said. He gathered up his kit.

Her grandfather had filled a small bucket with ice, and he grabbed the larger spit bucket. Cooper stopped to drape a towel over Jamie's shoulders to keep her warm.

"Need to get you a robe," he said.

She shrugged. Nerves were beating a tattoo in her belly. She felt as though she'd swallowed a bolt of lightning and the energy was crackling around inside her, desperate to find a way out.

Then they were walking the long corridor to the auditorium. She could hear the sound of the crowd, the music, the announcements.

Cooper held the door for her. She brushed past him and stepped into the bright circle of a spotlight that pinned her to the floor and tracked her as she made her way down the wide aisle to the ring. The crowd began to roar. She couldn't tell what they were yelling, but she could feel the energy of their attention and anticipation. The last two times she'd fought, she'd fed off the buzz of the crowd. Tonight she felt exposed, uncertain. They knew who she was now, who her father had been. They'd be watching, wondering.

The ring loomed before her. Cooper moved ahead to hold

the ropes open and she slid into the ring. She was alone on the canvas square, the glare of the lights and cameras and thousands of eyes on her as she danced from foot to foot. She rolled her shoulders, working to keep her breathing steady and even, despite the fact that every instinct was screaming at her to gasp for air and run, run, run.

The sound of the crowd intensified and she guessed that Liana was making her way to the ring. Jamie turned her back. The other woman would be posturing, showing off, trying to psych Jamie out some more. Deliberately, Jamie did a slow circuit of the ring, jogging from foot to foot as she mapped out her territory.

Even when Liana entered the ring she didn't give the other woman her attention. Right now, she was irrelevant. This time was about Jamie getting her head right, setting herself up to focus and think and act when the bell rang.

The MC began to make the announcements. Jamie noted that they'd changed her name from Holloway to Sawyer on the bill.

It was official. Her journey of redemption had begun.

"Jamie." Cooper gestured her toward her corner.

She crossed to him, keeping her feet moving, staying warm all the while. He handed her the mouthpiece, tugged the towel off her shoulders, checked her gloves again and smoothed a little more Vaseline onto her cheekbones. Then he grabbed her gloves and held her eye.

"You can do this. You've got the power, you've got the will, you've got the skill. Make it happen."

"Okay," she said. She felt as though she was making a promise or taking an oath.

Cooper hesitated a moment. Then he slapped a hand onto her shoulder and squeezed her once, firmly, before stepping away.

She sought her grandfather's face in the crowd beside the ring and found him standing to one side. He gave her a stern-faced nod of acknowledgement. She made him a mental promise: *For you, Grandpa. This one's for you.*

Then she turned around and took her first good, long look at her opponent. Liana Nelson was big and broad. She had rounded, muscular arms and a flat, wide face with hard pale green eyes framed by short, spiky blond hair. Abdominal muscles rippled down her belly, and her thighs and calves were thick with muscle.

She eyeballed Jamie straight back, her top lip curling into a sneer.

Jamie bumped her gloves together. She'd seen that sneer one too many times today. First chance she got, she was going to smack the hell out of it.

Kyle stood behind Liana's corner. Holding onto the ropes, he leaned forward and fed Liana last minute instructions. Jamie locked eyes with him briefly as he stepped down from the ring. Once, she'd let him screw her over. Tonight she was going to show him she was nobody's victim.

The ref called her into the center of the canvas. She stood quietly as he told them to keep the fight clean. Liana kept up her intense eye work. Jamie stayed cool. She could tell it pissed her opponent off.

Good.

They tapped gloves and retreated to their corners. Jamie caught sight of Cooper standing below, his arms crossed over his chest, his legs spread wide. He looked immovable, carved from granite. A hard man who'd won all his battles.

And he was on her side. It was a little scary to realize how much that meant to her. She turned back to face the ring and brought her fists up. Her breathing loud inside her own head, she waited for the bell to ring.

The reverberating clang seemed to hang forever in the air. Jamie moved forward, ready to take the fight up to her opponent. Liana met her halfway, fist first. Jamie blocked a jab to her face and a cross to her ribs before getting in a combination of her own. Liana's head rocked on her neck and she blinked quickly. Her green gaze took on a harder, angrier light. Pressing forward, Liana went on the attack. Jamie blocked as best she could, but it was impossible to deflect all her blows. Her head snapped back once, twice. She lost breath as her opponent's fist found her belly. Sucking air, Jamie shook her head. She forced the pain into the furthest corner of her mind. It was good for one thing and one thing only—keeping her focused, reminding her that this was a battle, and that only the strongest would survive.

Keeping her guard hand up, Jamie went on the attack again.

COOPER'S HANDS were fisted against his rib cage, his arms locked rigidly across his chest.

Even hearing that his boxing career was over felt like a walk in the park compared to watching Jamie get pounded with hit after hit. Everything in him wanted to bound into the ring and protect her from the blows raining down on her.

But this was boxing. This was what Jamie wanted. What she needed to purge her soul and fulfill her promise to her grandfather. Cooper had no choice but to sit back and watch and hope that she found what she was looking for inside the ring.

The crowd roared as Liana landed a strong jab on the side of Jamie's head. Jamie staggered, then threw herself straight back into the attack.

Cooper's shoulders tensed as Jamie concentrated on the other woman's body, pounding her with jabs and crosses, looking for an opening. Liana was fast and damned resilient. She bore up under the assault, closing the distance between them and grabbing Jamie in a clinch to stop her attack. The two women swayed, locked together in an angry, sweaty embrace. The ref stepped forward, ordering them to break. As Jamie relinquished her grip, Liana whipped a jab across the space that separated them, catching Jamie on the chin unaware.

Cooper bellowed with outrage. The ref shook his head and held up a hand to signal he was giving Liana a warning for a foul hit.

Jamie blinked. She shook her head, then once again took up her stance. Cooper felt a swell of pride. Tough and beautiful— no wonder she rocked his world.

By the time the first round bell sounded, Cooper calculated that Jamie was ahead on points, but only just.

This was going to be a close fight unless one of the women scored a knockout punch. He was in the ring beside Jamie in seconds, pushing her onto the stool. He accepted her mouth-piece and washed it out, then reached for the No-Swell and began to press it across her cheekbones.

"You're doing great. Keep riling her. Every time she gets angry, she wastes a lot of energy and she gets stupid."

Jamie nodded. She squirted water into her mouth then spat into the bucket. She had the beginnings of a bruise coming up on her left cheekbone, and a small cut on her lower lip. He cleaned the cut and slicked more Vaseline on as she sucked in big lungfuls of air.

"She's fast. And sneaky," she said.

"Dirty. But we knew that about her already," he said. With Vandenburg training her, there were no surprises. "Keep moving, keep popping up under her guard."

Their time was nearly up. He pushed her guard back into her mouth. Their eyes locked for a brief moment. He hoped like hell she couldn't see how much he wanted to sling her over his shoulder and drag her out of there.

I should have walked away.

He knew it with absolute clarity. He wasn't doing himself or Jamie any favors, feeling so torn when all his focus should be on keeping her in the zone and giving her the feedback and advice she so desperately needed.

The ref signaled. Cooper slipped back through the ropes, sliding the stool out after him. Arthur took the bucket and stool from him, placing them at the ready for the end of the next round.

The bell rang and Liana came after Jamie with ferocious

zeal, working her into a corner as she slammed punches into her shoulders, head, belly. The crowd surged to its feet, excited by the strong attack. Vandenburg crowed from the opposite corner. Cooper kept his focus on Jamie, willing her to stay strong. To endure.

Jamie slipped a shot in under the other woman's guard, then danced away. Liana came at Jamie again, her arms a blur of muscled motion as she struck and struck and struck. Again Jamie was driven into the corner.

Cooper wanted to look away but he couldn't let Jamie down just to spare himself.

Jamie let fly with another quick, fast shot, this time to Liana's belly. The other woman looked momentarily outraged that Jamie had once again gotten beneath her guard.

Dancing back to the center of the ring, Jamie grinned around her mouth guard and gestured toward Liana: *Come on, is that all you got?*

The crowd loved it. They were on their feet again, hollering their approval.

All finesse was forgotten as Liana stalked toward Jamie, shoulders bunched, head down low. Furious, she swung out at Jamie, and once again they wound up in the corner, Jamie trying to protect herself as best she could.

Liana was ahead on points by the time the bell sounded and Jamie came back to her corner.

Cooper squatted in front of her and held her chin with his hand to make sure he had her attention. Jamie's gaze focused on him, tired but determined. God, she was tough.

He waited while she rinsed and spat.

"How's your wind?" he asked.

She nodded, despite the fact she was gasping for air. "I'm okay."

"Good. You need to keep her moving, wear her out. She's not as fit as you. You can break her."

Jamie nodded again.

He shot a glance at the ref. It was time to let her go again. He wanted to say something, do something that would win the fight for her, save her all the pain that was yet to come.

But it wasn't his fight to win.

He slipped out of the ring as the bell rang. Once again both women came out fighting. They exchanged a flurry of blows. Jamie worked hard to outmaneuver her opponent, her feet a blur of motion as she danced around her. Liana tracked her around the ring, her chest heaving like a bellows, her gaze never wavering from her target. Then Jamie feinted with a left, and before she could move in with her right, Liana let fly with the whistling uppercut that had KO'd so many of her previous opponents. Jamie turned with it, tried to deflect it with her forearm. The other woman's glove smacked into the side of her jaw. Her eyes closed. Cooper braced himself to rush into the ring. Was she going down?

Jamie didn't fall. Instead, she stepped *toward* her opponent in a counterintuitive move that confused Liana and made her shuffle backward. Jamie delivered a sizzling haymaker with her right, the punch taking forever to swing around before slamming into the other woman's jaw with a resounding smack.

Liana's head lolled on her neck. Her knees buckled. Then she hit the canvas, out cold.

The ref bent over her, checking her eyes. He signaled with his hands that she was out. The crowd went crazy, yelling at the top of their lungs, chanting Jamie's name. Cooper dove for the ring. He slid between the ropes and scooped her into his arms, lifting her high.

She wrapped her legs around his waist and punched the air. She threw her head back, sweat spraying off her in glistening beads.

He'd won four championship bouts in his career, but no victory had ever felt as sweet. He'd wanted this for her so bad— both because he'd wanted the danger to be over, and because it meant so much to her.

They were both laughing and grinning like idiots. Then Arthur was there beside her. Cooper relinquished his grip on her. He watched as she hugged her grandfather, her face flushed with exertion and triumph.

The next few minutes passed in a blur as her win was officially announced and the crowd roared for her again. On their way back to the change room, Jamie was stopped by two different news crews for comments. She shrugged them off, refusing to feed them when they'd been prepared to tear her apart earlier. Then they were in her change room, the three of them high on relief and excitement.

Jamie was bright-eyed as she bounced from foot to foot, still hyped from the fight.

"I thought she had me that second time on the ropes," she said.

Cooper threw a towel around her shoulders and went to work on the tape holding her glove laces secure.

"She's a slugger, that's for sure. But she doesn't think enough. All power, no brain," he said, tugging the laces free.

"God, I feel so good."

Life didn't offer up many moments of pure triumph like this. He knew firsthand how high she was feeling right now. As though she could take on the world, all the aches and pains and bruises forgotten for a moment as she reveled in her victory.

Cooper tugged her gloves off, then grabbed her hands to keep them still as he unwound the tape protecting her knuckles.

"You get in the shower, and we'll go celebrate," Arthur said. He was grinning, fit to bust.

"Hell, yeah," Jamie said. She pulled away from Cooper's grip to kiss her grandfather again. "Let's go paint the town red."

Arthur slipped out the door into the corridor to offer Jamie privacy while she changed. Cooper reached for her hands again.

"Let me finish up and you can get in the shower," he said.

He could feel the energy vibrating through her as she watched him unwrap her hands.

"You think I'll have trouble getting another fight after this?"

"Are you kidding? Any female fighter with an ego is going to be lining up to try to knock down Jack Sawyer's daughter. Especially now that you've had such a splashy debut."

He was acutely aware of the heat coming off her body, the mingled scent of her clean sweat and deodorant and the massage oil he'd used on her earlier.

He felt an overwhelming desire to bury his face in her neck and suck her essence into his lungs. She infuriated him, she aroused him, she bemused him. Watching her get hit had been hell. Now he felt her joy, her triumph. He was so proud of her, so *damned* proud of her....

"Did you see the look she got in her eye when I popped that first shot under her guard? I thought she was going to pound me into the ground," Jamie said, her eyes unfocused and distant.

He'd denied himself last night, he'd been denying himself for weeks on end. He needed to hold her. To be with her. To be a part of her, even just for a few aching seconds.

He tossed the tape to one side and reached for her, sliding his hands up her neck and onto her skull so he could hold her head still as he lowered his mouth to hers. Her mouth opened beneath his hungrily and her tongue slid over his. She angled her head to allow him greater access. He could feel her whole body pounding with the force of her ramped-up heartbeat. His body was buzzing, too, from a heady mix of triumph, relief and desire.

Growling low in his throat, he backed her up until she was pressed against the cool tile wall. He reached for the lower edge of her sports crop. He had her out of her chest guard and bra in seconds, and he lowered his head to taste her, lick her, bite her. She started to lose it, grinding against him as she anticipated what was going to come next.

He pushed his hands inside the wide elastic on her fighting trunks and shoved them toward the floor, along with her underwear. Then he hooked one of her long legs over his hip.

His mouth devoured hers as he slid a questing hand into the slick heat between her thighs. She was wet and ready for him. Her whole body quivered as he pressed the flat of his palm against her.

"Cooper," she whispered desperately.

He was way ahead of her. He unbuckled his belt, then popped his button fly open.

Within seconds his rock-hard cock was pressed against her belly. He took care of protection, his hands shaking. Then he hitched her a little higher and guided himself between her thighs. He entered her with one long, powerful thrust. She gasped and closed her eyes.

"I have dreamed of this every night," she said, so low he almost couldn't hear her.

He began to move. He closed his eyes, reveling in how tight and hot she felt, how slickly their bodies moved together, how passionately she held him with her thighs and her strong arms.

"Yes," she whispered, her head thrown back. "Yes, Cooper."

It was so good, she was so good, he couldn't hold on. He gripped her hips and encouraged her to lift her other leg from the ground. He took her full weight as she wrapped both legs around him and locked her ankles behind his back. He pounded into her, teeth gritted, eyes closed, his whole body straining toward pleasure.

She was so beautiful, so brave, so sexy, so damned hot. The way her body gripped his, the slippery slide of her, the taste and smell and feel of her.

His climax slammed into him like a fist. He opened his eyes and stared at her as he poured himself into her. She was caught between agony and ecstasy as she rode her own orgasm. He squeezed her butt cheeks hard as he pumped one last time into her, feeling her inner muscles tightening again and again around him as they came simultaneously.

For a few seconds afterward there was nothing but the sound

of their harsh breathing in the change room. He rested his forehead against hers. She was trembling. He loosened his grip and withdrew from her, letting her legs slide to the ground.

Jamie's silver eyes were dark with satisfaction when he looked at her.

"That's what you get for holding out last night," she said, reaching out to cup him in her hand.

Because he was a man, and because he was staring at the sexiest woman he'd ever met, his cock immediately began to harden all over again.

She smiled a self-satisfied little smile. He started to respond when the door to the change room squeaked. He had just enough presence of mind to drag his jeans up over his bare butt and thrust a towel at Jamie before her grandfather stuck his head around the door.

"Shake a tail feather, Jimmy. This old man's hanging out for a beer," Arthur said before he saw them. Shock hit his features, followed quickly by a wave of color.

There was a moment of silent tension. Then Arthur cast Cooper a dark, disapproving look. He stepped backward without a word, letting the door fall shut behind him.

"Shit," Cooper said. He dragged his jeans together and buttoned his fly.

Jamie's cheeks were pink. She wrapped the towel around her body, tucking in the end between her breasts.

"Okay, that was embarrassing, but since this seems to keep happening, he was bound to find out sometime," she said.

Cooper buckled his belt.

"I can only imagine what he's thinking right now," he said.

He'd only known Arthur a few months, but he'd grown to respect the old man enormously. The way he looked out for Jamie, his fierce loyalty and his quiet presence all spoke of a man of his word, a man of honor.

The exact opposite of the kind of man who'd accept the role

of trusted trainer to a fighter then proceed to throw her on her back and stick it to her at every given opportunity.

"Like I said, he was always going to find out eventually," Jamie said. She headed for the shower.

Cooper made a rude noise. She gave him a knowing look over her shoulder.

"Until we get this thing out of our systems, it's going to keep happening, Cooper. You know it, and I know it. It's not a big deal, as long as we both remember what it is—and what it isn't."

He stared at the shower stall door as she closed it between them. A few months ago, having a woman as sexy as Jamie offer him no-strings sex would have been right up there with being offered a chance to come out of retirement with no risk of permanent injury. Problem was, sex with Jamie wasn't no-strings. Not for him, anyway.

He scrubbed his face with his hands. Bending, he collected the discarded tape and tidied up the rest of his kit. He could only procrastinate for so long. After a few minutes he braced himself and exited the change room.

He felt like a teenager who'd been busted jerking off over his mom's underwear drawer—dirty and downright wrong in so many ways. He'd known better. He'd tried to draw a line, but he hadn't been able to make it stick.

Arthur was standing with his hands shoved into his pockets. Slowly his focus swung around to fix on Cooper.

"How long has it been going on?"

"Long enough," Cooper said. "Not that it makes any difference, but I'm serious about Jamie."

Arthur's face was set. "You think I haven't heard that line before? She trusts you. She's put her whole career in your hands, and you repay her by diddling her at the first opportunity?"

Cooper shuffled his feet.

"You're right. I shouldn't have crossed the line and I know it. I'd already decided tonight to quit training her," he said. "I can't stand outside that ring and watch her take another beating. It's doing my head in."

He ran a hand through his hair, remembering again the urge he'd felt to stop the fight in its tracks and protect her. When he met Arthur's eyes again, the old man's expression was assessing.

"She needs a trainer more than she needs a boyfriend. Got them lined up around the block," Arthur said.

Cooper shrugged. He felt the way he felt. And he'd already tried to pull back to being only Jamie's trainer. It wasn't going to happen.

"I'll hook her up with someone. She's got a record now, and the Sawyer name is bound to attract some interest," he said.

"She won't like trading on the name."

But they both knew that horse had well and truly bolted.

"Does she know? About you not training her any more?" Arthur asked.

"No."

Jamie was so driven, so intent on proving herself that there was no room in her life for doubt or other people's mixed motives or feelings. He'd already tried to explain to her how much their sexual attraction compromised their professional relationship. She didn't want to hear it.

Tonight she was going to have to listen.

He stared at the change room door. She would be angry. But there was no other way. He cared too much. He wanted her too badly.

The question was, once their working relationship was cleared up, would she acknowledge their personal one? Or was he going to have yet another battle on his hands?

9

JAMIE STEPPED OUT of the shower and pressed her face into her towel. She winced for the tenth time in as many minutes as she remembered the look on her grandfather's face.

It was useless to pretend that him finding her buck naked and pink with afterglow was not cause for just a little bit of self-consciousness. But it had happened, and in a way she was glad.

The attraction she felt for Cooper was not going to go away with a few rolls in the hay. Despite their best intentions, they kept winding up naked and sweaty with each other.

It couldn't last, of course. That kind of desire never did. Equally, it wasn't fading of its own accord. The past few months had more than proven that.

Which left her and Cooper in a quandary. After tonight, more than ever, she knew she needed Cooper as her trainer. He'd grounded her when she'd been ready to walk, he'd focused her, he'd given her confidence. With him in her corner, she felt rock-solid.

There was only one solution: they needed to burn this thing out. Just go at it until they were bored or tired or over each other. A week, two weeks, a month. Whatever it took. She honestly couldn't see any other way around it.

He would get on his high horse again, no doubt. He had some pretty old-fashioned views about the trust that should exist between a fighter and a trainer. She liked that about him a hell of a lot but it didn't solve the problem of their mutual attraction. Only overexposure was going to do that. Once they'd sated each other's desire, sex would be a nonissue and they could get back to what counted.

Jamie smoothed her hands down her slim-fit jeans and inspected her face. Her lower lip was puffy from Liana Nelson's powerful left jab, and her right eye was starting to turn purple with a bruise.

God, she'd won.

She closed her eyes and relived the moment when the final bell had sounded. Just like last time, it had brought a heady rush. Winning was addictive. She wanted more of it—soon. Maybe she *was* her father's daughter.

She pulled her hair into a ponytail then turned away from the mirror, her mouth tight. Her father had no place in any of this. She was annoyed with herself for thinking of him.

Stowing the rest of her gear in her gym bag, she prepared to face her grandfather. He would have things to say, no doubt, about her and Cooper. But she was a grown woman, and she was entitled to do what she wanted with whomever she wanted. Maybe it was the high from her win, but tonight she didn't feel as though there was any problem that was insurmountable.

Both men were waiting for her in the corridor. Neither of them quite met her eye. Fine. A few beers and a good meal would take care of any awkwardness.

"Let's go. There's a pub within walking distance of the motel that looks like it has a good dinner menu," she said.

She waited until they'd pulled up out the front of the pub before turning to face Cooper and her grandfather.

"Let's get this out of the way so we can all have a good time, okay?" she said. She looked her grandfather in the eye. "Cooper and I like each other. It doesn't mean anything. I'm sorry you had to find out like that, but there's not much I can do about it now. Okay?"

Her grandfather eyed her steadily.

"Cooper's your trainer, Jimmy. What you're doing together messes things up. You need to be able to rely on each other."

Jamie opened her mouth to tell her grandfather that sex was nothing but a bunch of body parts rubbing together and that it wouldn't mess up anything. She closed it again without saying a word. She might be a grown woman, but there was no way she could have that conversation with her grandfather.

"Cooper and I understand each other," she said. "Don't worry about it."

Her grandfather shot Cooper a look. She suspected he'd been giving Cooper a hard time while she changed. Cooper was a big boy, he could handle it.

"Come on. I'm thirsty," she said.

She led the way inside. The Royal Standard was a classic Australian country pub with a long wooden counter along one wall, booths along another and a collection of tables and chairs filling the bulk of the floor space. Local memorabilia served as decoration, and in one corner a television showed highlights from the day's football matches. The menu was written in colored chalk on a blackboard behind the bar.

Jamie marched straight up to the counter and ordered three beers. Technically, champagne was probably called for, but she'd always been more of a beer girl and she was willing to bet Cooper and her grandfather were the same.

She carried three frosty glasses back to the table Cooper had chosen, sliding a beer toward each of them and raising her own glass.

"To laying Nelson out," she said.

The wary look left her grandfather's eyes as he remembered the fight.

"That sure was a beautiful shot you popped her," he said wistfully.

They all took a drink, then Cooper raised his glass.

"To Jamie, for fighting like a champion against the odds. You did great," he said.

Warmth filled her chest at the approval, respect and admiration she saw in his face.

Talk became more natural after that as they rehashed the fight. Her grandfather crowed over the look on Kyle Vandenburg's face when Liana had gone down.

"Wish I'd had a camera," he said with a rueful shake of his head. "A-hole."

They ordered another round of beers and a meal each. By the time they'd pushed their plates away, the mood was mellow.

Jamie was confident that any awkwardness had been dealt with. There was still some residual tension with Cooper, but they would sort that out. This time, they'd do it her way, and not his. Abstinence was not a viable prospect between the two of them. Cooper was going to have to face the fact, get over it and move on.

"Well, I think that's it for me," her grandfather said, pushing himself back from the table. "These old bones are calling for bed."

Jamie checked the clock on the wall. It was barely ten o'clock.

"You're kidding, right? We're just getting started."

Her grandfather shot Cooper a meaningful look. "I'm tired. It was a big day. And I'm sure you two have things to talk about."

Kissing her on the cheek, he headed for the door. She followed him with her eyes until the door swung shut on him. She turned to Cooper.

"What was that supposed to mean?"

Cooper turned his glass around and around on his beer mat. Then he looked her in the eye.

"I'm not going to train you anymore, Jamie."

She'd been half expecting this. She rolled her eyes.

"Honestly, you and my grandfather should go polish your suits of armor together. It's just sex, Cooper. You haven't exploited me or taken advantage of me or let me down. Quitting as my trainer would be letting me down."

She leaned across the table and slid a hand behind his neck. Pulling him close, she angled her mouth over his and kissed him long and slow. His eyes were smoky with desire when she pulled away.

Damn, but this man did it for her.

"We have great sexual chemistry, and that's been a distraction. We just need to get it out of our systems, burn it out," she said. "A few weeks of letting nature take its course and it won't be an issue anymore."

She curled her fingers into his hair and leaned closer for another kiss. This time Cooper pulled away.

"You're not listening to me. I can't train you anymore. I should never have taken you on in the first place when I was so hot for you. I'll find you someone else—Bob Godfrey, Gary Bedford. Either of them would be great for you."

She frowned. Why was he so hell bent on being Mr. Bloody Honorable over this?

"Cooper, I don't blame you, if that's what you're worried about. We both did this. And we're both adults. Sleeping with each other is not the end of the world."

"Jesus, Jamie. Do you have any idea how hard it was for me watching you in that ring tonight? I was nervous for you, I was damned near sick for you. I wanted to rip Vandenburg's head off and slap Liana Nelson down and step into that ring and save your ass."

"My ass doesn't need to be saved," she said.

"I get that. And I get that you don't want to hear that I have feelings for you, and that you think sex is just sex and all that bull. But here's the thing, Jamie—I like you. A lot. I think about you, I dream about you, I want more from you than mindless humping. I want to see what else there might be between us other than great sex."

Just like last night, her back came up. She didn't want to hear this from him. She didn't want him to feel anything for her. Scowling, she knocked back more of her beer.

"I don't do relationships," she said.

"I'm not Vandenburg," he said. "I'm not going to screw you over, Jamie."

She flinched. She hated that he knew about her weak past.

"If I have to choose between having sex with you and having you as a trainer, I choose the trainer," she said.

"You don't get that option anymore, it's off the table."

She stared at him. He was dead serious about this. Then she remembered her grandfather. Cooper respected her grandfather. This was obviously a bout of self-flagellation after being caught with his pants down.

"If this is because my grandfather caught us, it doesn't matter," she said. "He'll get over it."

Cooper leaned forward, his body tense.

"Listen to what I'm saying and stop trying to make it about something else. I care about you, Jamie Sawyer. That's why I can't be your trainer anymore. I care too much to watch you get hurt."

"I don't want you to care. I don't want any of this," she said. She sounded like a scared kid, but she couldn't take the words back.

Cooper reached out, his hands cupping her face with infinite tenderness. He drew her close for a kiss. His lips brushed hers gently, delicately. Then he slid his tongue into her mouth. She could taste the desire in him, the sincerity, the emotion. Something deep inside her rose up in response. She found herself reaching for him, clutching at his shoulders as she lost control for a few seconds.

He was a good man, an honest man. He'd always been straight with her. She loved the way he made her laugh, and the way he ran his gym and spoke to his staff, and she admired the hell out of his grit and determination and self-respect. He had an amazing body, and sometimes when he touched her she felt so beautiful and desirable it made her soul ache….

She gasped and pushed him away.

The last time she'd been stupid enough to fall in love, Kyle Vandenburg had screwed her over and tossed her aside. She could still remember the day she'd gone to his house with the letters from the debt collectors, trying to find some explanation for what had happened other than that he'd let her down. He hadn't even let her past the doorstep. He'd simply told her he couldn't help her. Shit happened, he'd said. Investments fall through, people are unreliable. She'd started to cry, unable to fully comprehend that this was the same man who had shared her bed for over a year and held her at night when she anguished over her father. To her shame, she'd even begged him to tell her why he was doing this to her.

She should have known the answer: because he could. Because he was a professional fighter, a predator, and his need to conquer extended outside the ring to everything in his life. He'd had her, he'd grown bored of her. Her financial affairs had become messy and embarrassing. It was time to move on.

Cooper wasn't like Kyle. Her heart knew that, as well as her gut. But she never wanted to feel that vulnerable again. Because people *were* unreliable. Kyle. Her father.

Something heavy and dark pressed down on her chest. She blinked rapidly. She looked after herself now, relying on no one. The only person she trusted was her grandfather.

"This is about more than sex," Cooper said. He reached for her, but she flinched away from him.

"I don't want to have feelings for you. Don't you get that?" she asked. "I don't want to care."

"It's too late, Jamie. We're already friends. We're lovers. We care about each other. When I kiss you, I know it's more than sex that's driving us. I can feel it." He tapped his chest with two fingers.

She stared at him. "Since when did you become the expert on emotions? I bet you've never had a long-term relationship in your life. I bet you've screwed your way across the States and all the way around Australia," she said.

"Yep. Just like I bet you've slept with men when you wanted sex, too," he countered. "That's why I know this is real. That it counts for something. That it's worth exploring."

It was true. She'd never felt this way with any of the other men she allowed into her bed. Not the hot, insatiable desire, not the need to be with him, not the thrill when their glances caught, not the warmth that spread through her chest and belly when she heard him laugh or he threw a word of praise her way. That was all for Cooper, only for Cooper.

She shoved her chair away from the table, distancing herself from him.

"Fine. You're not my trainer anymore," she said, sitting back and crossing her arms. "Thank you for everything you've done for me so far. Thanks for a good time. Have a nice life."

There was a long silence as he stared at her. She raised her eyebrows and stared back.

"What were you expecting to hear? I'm not going to say I have feelings for you, Cooper. I like having sex with you. You have a great body and a beautiful cock. End of story. If I had the choice again, I'd say no to the sex and keep you as a trainer."

Cooper stood and reached for his wallet. Without a word, he threw money down for the tab and slid his wallet into his back pocket. Then he turned and headed for the door.

She forced herself to watch him go. Only when he'd disappeared from sight did she realize that she had a white-knuckle hold on the edge of the table.

She took a deep breath and released her grip. She couldn't quite believe that he'd walked away from her. Even right up until the last few moments, she'd hoped that she could talk him around.

She'd just been hitting her stride. She'd found her training groove, understood what he expected from her, what they were aiming for together. She liked his sense of humor, the succinct way he offered criticism and suggestions for improvements to her technique. They'd won tonight against a fighter with vastly more experience. They made a good team.

She swore under her breath. Reaching for her beer, she downed the last of it in one big swallow. Just when she'd taken the first major step in her boxing career, he'd walked away from her.

For all his fancy talk about not being like Kyle, about the relationship between a trainer and fighter being about trust, he'd let her down. Just like the rest of them.

She didn't want him to *care* for her. She wanted a relationship with him on *her* terms—a relationship she could keep at arm's length and control. A relationship that wasn't going to leave her raw and hurting and broken.

Screw him.

She slammed her empty beer glass down onto the table. Crossing to the bar, she ordered a straight vodka. The bartender slid it toward her and she sucked back a fiery mouthful. She settled onto a stool and propped her elbows on the bar.

There were other trainers out there. She didn't need Cooper. She certainly didn't want what he was offering her—whatever the hell it was. The chance to "explore" the feelings between them—not interested, thanks for calling. Next, please.

An hour passed. She was on her third straight vodka when a group of a dozen or so people breezed into the pub. She didn't pay them any mind until one of them propped beside her at the bar. After a few beats she turned her head to look at him.

"What do you want?" she asked Kyle.

"To buy you a drink. That was a good show you put on tonight, Jimmy," he said.

"No."

Behind him, she could see the crowd he'd come in with had taken over two booths along the back wall. Liana Nelson was among them. Her green gaze bored into Jamie from across the room.

Someone was a bad loser.

"Come on, for old times' sake," Kyle said. He leaned a little closer. "We had plenty of good times before things went sour, Jimmy."

She stared at him, taking in his confident smile and good looks. Once, she had loved him.

"Not if I was dying of thirst," she said very clearly. She turned her gaze to the television screen in the corner of the bar.

Kyle laughed and reached out to touch her. She caught his wrist before he even came close. Five years of buried rage and grief burned its way up her chest and into her throat as she glared at him.

"I'm not twenty-two anymore, Kyle, and I know how to look after myself. Believe me, you don't want to take me on." She let his wrist go. "Now, which part of piss off don't you understand?"

The smile dropped from his lips and his I'm-a-good-guy demeanor slipped at last.

"You always did think you were too good for me," he said. "With your private school education and your fancy BMW that daddy bought you."

She stared at him.

"Is that why you screwed me over? Because of the school I went to?"

Kyle's mouth worked for a beat, as though he was trying to decide whether to say something or not.

"I asked your father for a loan once, when I was just starting out. Do you know what he told me? *It's good for fighters to be hungry, Kyle.*"

"My father didn't believe in hand outs. He thought it was good for a fighter to need to win as well as want it."

Was it possible that Kyle was really that petty? That her

father's actions and his own sense of inferiority and entitlement had led him to betray her all those years ago?

"Yeah? Well, you tell me, Jamie. How does it feel to be the hungry one for a change? How's that working out for you?"

There was so much bitterness in him that she had to look away. She signaled to the bartender to hit her with another vodka.

"What, nothing to say now that the boot's on the other foot?" Kyle said.

"That's right. I have nothing to say to someone who's so feeble he blames his own weaknesses on someone else. You were always spending more than you earned, even when you started winning big. You always wanted the best, even if you couldn't afford it. Don't you dare blame my father or me because you couldn't live up to your own expectations. Now, if you don't mind, I was enjoying myself up until about five minutes ago."

She turned away from him, reaching for her vodka. She was aware of his anger, of the potential for violence that hung between them, but she kept her gaze fixed straight ahead.

After a long moment, Kyle pushed away from the bar and swiveled on his heel, returning to his posse.

Her shoulders relaxed.

She should go, but she didn't want him to think he'd scared her away.

She frowned as she paid for her vodka. She couldn't believe that his exploitation of her and her family had come down to something so small and simple. How had he become so resentful, so envious, that he'd seen her father's fall from grace as an opportunity to even the score?

"If you know what's good for you, you'll stay away from him."

Jamie looked up to see Liana Nelson looming over her. The other woman was sporting a black eye and a bruised jaw from where Jamie had knocked her out.

"Relax. He's all yours. I wouldn't take him if he came with a million bucks tied around his neck with a bow," Jamie said.

"He told me about you, how your family blames him for the way your father screwed up your lives," Liana said. "Poor little daddy's girl who couldn't make it on her own."

Jamie clenched her hand around the glass. She'd never had a fight outside of the dojo or the ring, but right at that moment she was experiencing an almost irresistible urge to push the other woman's teeth down her throat.

Except that was exactly what Liana wanted.

"You want a rematch, you talk to my trainer," Jamie said.

Then she remembered that she didn't have a trainer. She pushed her vodka away. She was starting to feel distinctly sorry for herself, which meant it was time to go back to the motel.

"You got lucky," Liana said, leaning in close.

Anger radiated off her. Jamie slid off her stool so they were standing eye-to-eye.

"I won. Suck it up."

She headed for the door without a backward glance.

Outside, the night air was warm and dusty. She took a moment to blink and get her bearings in the darkness of the parking lot. Technically, she was probably a little drunk. But the walk back to the motel would help clear her head.

She was barely halfway across the asphalt lot when she heard the pub door open behind her. She knew without turning who it was and what was about to happen. So much for never having had a fight outside the ring.

"Sawyer," Liana called.

Jamie stopped but didn't turn around. "Just let it go, Liana."

"What's the matter? Don't think you can get lucky twice?" Liana asked.

Jamie set her jaw. This woman was beginning to really piss her off. Despite her win, it had been a pretty shitty night. Between Cooper's abandonment, her grandfather's disapproval, Kyle's smugness and Liana's prodding, she didn't see how it could get much worse.

"Why the hell not?" she muttered.

Maybe it was the vodka. Maybe it was watching Cooper walk away. Maybe it was a whole bunch of stuff that had been piling up in the back of her mind for too long.

She turned around. Kyle and his friends had followed Liana out of the bar. Great, they had an audience.

"You want a piece of me?" she asked Liana, squaring up. "Come and get it."

COOPER WATCHED the taillights of a passing car fade into the distance as he approached the pub on foot.

He'd been about to head to bed when Arthur had come knocking on his door. The old man had been concerned that Jamie hadn't returned to the motel yet. Like the sap he was, Cooper had offered to go look for her. Chivalry, it seemed, was not entirely dead, even in Dubbo late on a Saturday night.

As he rounded the fence line and approached the pub's parking lot, he saw a huddle of people in the corner and heard hooting and catcalls. He'd been in enough street brawls to recognize the signs. He steered around them, not wanting to get sucked into something that was none of his business.

Then he caught sight of the two combatants. Adrenaline squeezed his gut.

Liana Nelson was going at Jamie. Any finesse she'd possessed in the ring fell by the wayside as she got stuck into Jamie's ribs and belly. Jamie was covering and blocking the best she could, but he could see she was hurting. Bare-knuckle fighting was a hell of a lot more painful than boxing with gloves on, and a hell of a lot more dangerous.

"Jesus," he muttered, striding forward.

He was on the outer rim of the circle of spectators and pushing his way through when a big, brawny shoulder blocked his way.

"Let them sort it out," Kyle Vandenburg said.

"Get out of my way," Cooper said.

"My girl deserves a rematch."

Cooper's gaze slid over Vandenburg's shoulder. Liana was taking shots at Jamie's face, trying to hurt her as much as possible. A bright streak of red bled down from Jamie's nose and across her mouth. Something primitive went off in Cooper's brain. He elbowed his way past the other man, forcing his way into the circle. In two strides he was on Liana, hauling her off Jamie and shoving her away.

"Back off," he warned in a low, intense growl.

Jamie stumbled and lifted a forearm to wipe at her face. She looked surprised to see blood smeared up her arm. He couldn't tell if she was punch-drunk or just drunk-drunk. Now didn't really seem the time to worry about it.

"Let's get out of here," he said, grabbing her hand.

Vandenburg blindsided Cooper with a jab to the jaw before he'd taken his first step toward the motel. His head snapped back and pain radiated up the side of his face. Quickly Cooper shuffled back to get out of Vandenburg's range.

The other man squared up, his teeth bared in a feral grin. Out of the corner of his eye, Cooper could see Liana circling in on Jamie again. Not taking his eyes off Vandenburg, Cooper reached behind himself and grabbed Jamie's arm.

"Stay behind me," he said.

Vandenburg feinted forward, throwing a cross. Cooper ducked around it, firing a quick one-two into the other man's ribs. Vandenburg fell back a step, and Cooper glanced at Jamie. Liana was coming at her again, throwing punches. Jamie danced around her, her boots rasping loudly on the asphalt, her breath coming fast.

Then he was too busy defending himself against Vandenburg, ducking shots, weaving. Concentrating on body shots, he rained blows down on Vandenburg. It didn't take long for the sneaky son of a bitch to try a knee in Cooper's balls, then a gouge to the eye. Cooper thumped him hard in the kidneys in retaliation.

Getting a good grip on the other man's shoulders, he shoved him backward so forcefully that Vandenburg fell on his ass.

Cooper checked on Jamie. Liana had a handful of her hair, and Jamie ignored everything he'd ever taught her and rammed her knee into the other woman's torso. The scratch of gravel underfoot told him Vandenburg was on his feet again. Before he turned away he saw Jamie land a punch square in the other woman's face. The crunch of bone breaking was audible from ten feet away. Liana dropped to her knees, blood gushing from her nose.

Cooper brought up his guard as he faced Vandenburg.

"Liana's down. Don't you want to see to her?" he suggested. His breath was coming hard and fast.

"She can look after herself," Vandenburg said, spitting bloody saliva to one side.

"You always were a stupid bastard," Cooper said as he moved in for the kill.

Ruthless, he slammed a fist into the side of Vandenburg's neck. It was an old street-fighting technique, and it sent Vandenburg to his knees, gasping for breath.

Game over.

Wiping his bloodied knuckles on his jeans, Cooper turned to look for Jamie. She was hunkered down on a nearby curb, trying to catch her breath. Liana was being attended to by one of her friends, a bloody T-shirt held to her face.

"Think I broke her nose," Jamie said. She shook her right hand as though it hurt.

She had a cut across the bridge of her nose, a fat lip and one of her eyes was badly swollen.

"Let's get you home," he said. He held out a hand to pull her to her feet.

She reached out to take it. Then her gaze slid over his shoulder and her eyes widened with fear.

"Cooper!" she screamed.

He started to turn. He was too late. Something hard and heavy slammed into his skull.

Quicker than he could ever imagine, the world went blacker than black.

10

JAMIE WOKE WITH a crick in her neck from sleeping curled across three waiting room chairs. Rolling into a seated position, she rested her head in her hands and scrubbed her face with her palms.

The stunning blow to the head that Vandenburg had delivered with a stray piece of metal piping had given Cooper a concussion. It had also torn the retina away from his bad eye again. The doctors at Dubbo had been reluctant to operate on such a complicated injury, especially given Cooper's medical history. He'd been airlifted to the Sydney Eye Hospital the moment he had been deemed fit for transfer. Her grandfather had driven her back to Sydney in Cooper's four-wheel drive as soon as the hospital chopper had left. She'd paced the hospital corridors for hours ever since, waiting for word on Cooper's condition.

She hadn't been allowed in to see him. She wasn't family, she wasn't anything to him. So far she'd only gleaned the barest information: he'd had a restless night, and first thing this morning he'd gone into surgery. He'd been under the surgeon's knife for five hours. Five long, dark, terrifying hours.

She'd sent her grandfather home long ago. He'd been pale and shrunken with fatigue and she'd insisted he go, firmly ushering him into a taxi.

She checked the wall clock. Enough time had passed for her to ask after Cooper's condition again. There was a new nurse on the desk, a younger woman. She frowned when Jamie stopped in front of the nurse's station.

Jamie had a fair idea what she was staring at; when she'd examined herself blearily in the ladies' bathroom at 5:00 a.m. this morning, she'd been shaken by her own appearance. She could only imagine what the other woman was thinking.

"I'm sorry, but Emergency is the next level down," the nurse said.

"I'm fine. I just wanted to check and see if Cooper Fitzgerald is out of surgery yet."

"I see. Can I ask what your relationship to Mr. Fitzgerald is?" the nurse asked.

Jamie took a deep breath and reached for patience. Couldn't these people see that she was dying inside, waiting to find out if Cooper was going to be all right, if his life was going to be blighted because of her?

"He's my trainer. I'm a boxer," she explained, as she had several times over the past few hours. "Please. I need to know he's all right."

The nurse looked torn. Then her expression softened.

"Give me a minute," she said.

She disappeared. Jamie rested her aching head in her hand. When the nurse returned, she was accompanied by a short, gray-haired man wearing a doctor's coat.

"You were asking after Mr. Fitzgerald?" he said.

Jamie waited for the usual brush-off, but to her surprise he took her gently by the elbow and steered her toward the chairs where she'd been waiting.

"I'm Dr. Samuels. I take it you're Jamie? He's been asking after you," the doctor explained.

She ignored how much her stupid heart swelled at his words and concentrated on what mattered.

"Is he going to be okay? Was the surgery successful?"

She allowed him to guide her into a seat.

"The operation was complicated because this is the second time he's suffered an extensive detachment, but all the signs are good so far."

"So far. What does that mean?" she asked. Her hands gripped her knees tightly.

"It means that with eye surgery there are always risks. There are complications that may arise in a few days' time that we might have to deal with. But at the moment he's had the best treatment possible and he's resting comfortably."

Jamie swallowed the hot rush of tears that clogged the back of her throat.

She would never, ever forget the image of Kyle swinging that length of pipe down on Cooper's head, or the way Cooper's body had crumpled, his knees buckling, his head lolling on his neck. The memory of it alone was enough to make her feel sick and weak. She'd lunged forward in time to cushion Cooper's head before it hit the ground, but it had been too little, too late.

"My major concern at the moment is Mr. Fitzgerald's agitation. He keeps asking after you, wanting to know if you're okay," Dr. Samuels said, his brown eyes scanning her battered face.

Jamie shrugged, as she had every time one of the hospital staff suggested she seek treatment for her injuries.

"I'm fine," she said.

"How about we let me be the judge of that? I'd like to take a look at you. That way I can assure Mr. Fitzgerald that you are in one piece and largely uninjured."

Jamie opened her mouth to object. Then she thought of Cooper. If he was genuinely worried about her, being offered reassurance might help him rest.

"Okay. Whatever," she said gracelessly.

The doctor led her to an examination room where he checked her over briskly, testing her pupils and other reflexes, examining her hand, palpating her stomach.

"That's a nasty eye you have there, but I don't think you've sustained any permanent damage. And the hand is bruised rather than broken, fortunately."

"Can I see him?" she asked.

"He's sleeping off the anesthetic still."

"I don't care. I need to see for myself that he's all right."

Dr. Samuels checked his watch.

"Just a few minutes, then. But I'd like you to go home and get some rest yourself, put some ice on that eye."

"When can he go home? What happens next?" she asked, stubbornly concentrating on Cooper.

"He's going to be effectively blind for the next few days. If he wants to go home, there's no medical reason why he can't do so tomorrow. But he will require full-time help. He may wish to remain in the hospital. Many patients do."

Not Cooper. She knew that without asking. He would hate to be anywhere where he felt more powerless and weak than he had to. She knew, because that was exactly how she would feel.

The examination over, Dr. Samuels led her along the corridor to a private room. He held the door open for her.

"Two minutes," he warned.

"Yes. Thank you. I appreciate you bending the rules for me," she said.

He gave her a faint, kind smile and she slid past him. The room was dark, the curtains drawn over the window. Only a small light directly over the bed was on. Cooper's dark hair stood out starkly against the white of the sheets. His eyes were bandaged shut, a thick pad of gauze resting over his left eye. A drip fed into his right arm. The only sound was the faint hush of his breathing and her own heartbeat pounding in her ears.

She was afraid to touch him. He was in this condition because of her. Because she hadn't walked away from Liana's stupid challenge. Because she'd been angry and frustrated about not getting what she wanted from Cooper, and angry and frustrated because he'd asked for something from her that she'd been unable—unwilling—to give.

"I'm so sorry," she whispered. Tentatively she reached out to touch his arm.

His skin felt warm and familiar. She curled her fingers around his forearm.

If he'd died...

She couldn't complete the thought.

She stared down into his face.

"Please be all right," she said, low and intense.

The door opened behind her.

"Jamie," Dr. Samuels said.

She wanted to tell him to go to hell.

Instead, she lowered her head and kissed Cooper's bruised knuckles, brushing her hand up his forearm in one final caress. Then she left the room and the hospital and went home.

He'd need a home nurse to make it possible for him to leave the hospital tomorrow. As soon as she swung in the front door, she grabbed the phone book from beneath the kitchen counter and reached for the phone.

Her grandfather came in from the bedroom, tying the sash on his dressing gown.

"How is he?"

"Out of surgery. The doctor said it went well, and that he can come home tomorrow. I'm organizing a nurse for him," she said. Her finger was already running down the column of advertisements in the phone book.

She could feel her grandfather watching her. She ignored him and reached for the phone.

"Did you get yourself checked out?" he asked.

"I'm okay. A couple of bruises."

She picked an agency at random and called, explaining the situation. The woman asked a series of questions—was twenty-four-hour coverage required, would it be a live-in role, what was the location? Jamie realized she didn't even know where Cooper lived.

Her mind racing, she apologized to the woman and told her she would call her back with the details. Then she phoned Ray.

"I need Cooper's home address," she said.

"Jimmy! Man, I have been trying and trying to get through to you on your cell phone. What a fight, girl! Have you seen the papers? You're all over the place," he said.

Jamie frowned, confused. *Fight? Papers?* How had the media got hold of Cooper's story so quickly?

Then she remembered her bout last night, being outed as a Sawyer, the media scramble. It all seemed so distant and unimportant now.

"Listen, Ray, I really can't talk. I just need Cooper's address," she repeated.

Bemused, Ray reeled it off to her. Jamie jotted it down, called back the agency, then scooped up Cooper's car keys again.

"Where are you going?" her grandfather asked.

"To Cooper's place. I need to make sure he's got everything he needs for when he comes home," she said.

"You can do that later. You're exhausted. Grab some shut-eye. Cooper's house will still be there in a few hours' time."

She shook her head. She had to do this before she did anything else.

"At least have a shower, get rid of those bloody clothes." Her grandfather's voice was rough with frustration and concern.

Jamie looked down at herself. The knee was ripped out of her jeans, and blood and dirt were smeared across the front of her top.

She didn't care. The only thing that mattered was Cooper, making him comfortable, making things right for him.

"I'm fine," she said. It was becoming a mantra, she'd said it so often to so many different people today.

Her grandfather made a disgruntled noise but she ignored him and swung out the door. Cooper's house was in Annandale, only five minutes' drive from her own apartment. She tapped her fingers impatiently against the steering wheel the whole way. She'd taken two days off work for the fight, the Friday and Monday, to make a four-day weekend. Today was Sunday, so she had two whole days to get Cooper settled.

She made a mental list of the chores she would tackle. She would change Cooper's bed and make sure he had clean sheets and towels to come home to, stock up his fridge and pantry with groceries. She'd pack a bag for him so he could leave the hospital in his own clothes, and she'd make sure that the staff at the gym knew what was going on.

Following Ray's directions, she pulled up in front of a gracious, wide two-story Victorian terrace house. Painted a sandstone color, it had shiny black shutters and was surrounded by lush tropical landscaping. Barely sparing a glance for any of it, she let herself inside.

Polished floorboards and clean cream walls greeted her in the hallway. She ducked first into a spacious formal living room, furnished with warm modern furniture in dark brown leather. The dining room was next, then a granite and stainless steel kitchen opening onto a spacious casual living zone. Realizing there were no bedrooms downstairs, she made her way upstairs and found his bedroom. At the front of the house, it featured a king-size bed and smelled of Cooper.

Clothes were discarded in the corner, and the quilt was thrown back on his bed as though he'd rolled out of it and never looked back. There was still an indent on his pillow from where his head had rested. She curved her hand into it as she took in his most private space. Photos from his boxing career filled the walls on either side of the windows, stylish black-and-white shots in thick, square black frames. The carpet was dark chocolate-brown, and his bedroom furniture was simple—a walnut headboard and clean-lined tables with old-fashioned swing-arm lamps on either side of the bed. His quilt cover was wide wale corduroy in a rich coffee color, and his sheets were dark chocolate, the same as the carpet. It was a man's room, unpretentious, masculine, simple. Most importantly, it was Cooper's.

She swayed on her feet, weariness catching up with her. Shaking herself awake, she searched through his cupboards until she found his sheets. She stripped the bed, remade it, fluffed his pillows and carried the other sheets downstairs to the laundry. Unable to stop, she shoved them into the washing machine and turned it on. Then she turned to the kitchen. By the time she'd returned from the supermarket, the washing was done. She put it on to dry. Only when she'd packed away the groceries and run out of other tasks to occupy her did she come to a halt in the middle of Cooper's rear living room.

She couldn't think of a single other thing to do except wait and hope.

She closed her eyes. Her chin wobbled in a way that it hadn't since she was a very little girl.

She took a deep, shaky breath. This wasn't the time to indulge herself.

He had to be all right. He had to regain his sight. He had to walk away from this as whole as he'd been before he'd come back to save her from herself.

Sinking onto the couch, she held a cushion to her chest and gripped it hard. She was so tired, a weariness that went more than bone deep.

Promising herself she would steal only a few minutes' sleep, she lay down. Curled on her side, she closed her eyes.

When she next woke, clear morning light was pouring in the rear windows. She sat bolt upright and checked the time on the microwave in the kitchen. It was nearly 9:00 a.m. She'd slept around the clock.

Her mouth felt disgusting, her hand still ached and there was a feeling of heaviness around her bad eye. Apart from those minor concerns, she felt clearheaded for the first time since the attack.

She walked into Cooper's kitchen. The overnight bag she'd packed for him sat waiting in the hallway. A long supermarket receipt was curled on the counter. Flowers filled the vase she'd found under his sink yesterday.

She pressed a hand to her mouth as she suddenly realized what she'd done—invaded Cooper's home and life without any thought for how he might feel.

Cooper had told her that he cared for her. That was all. And on that single, tentative declaration, she'd taken over his life as though she had a right to be the one to look after him.

She took a step toward the vase. Then she stopped and shook her head.

She couldn't undo the things that she'd done. Any of them, good or bad.

Her hand curled into a fist. When Cooper discovered all that she'd done for him, he'd know that she cared for him.

It scared her almost as much as it filled her with hope.

She grabbed the car keys and collected the overnight bag. When she stepped onto the front porch, she saw the newspaper rolled up on the doorstep. She walked past it, not interested. They'd have the story of Cooper's assault by now. She hoped like hell the newspapers hadn't tracked him to the hospital yet. Running the gauntlet of the press was the last thing Cooper needed.

She stopped by her own apartment only long enough to reassure her grandfather, shower and change clothes before she drove to the hospital. To her relief, there were no crowds of photographers and reporters hovering. The smallest of blessings.

She could hear Cooper from the corridor as she approached his room. She closed her eyes in relief at the firm, uncompromising note in his voice. Surely he wouldn't be throwing his weight around if he was truly ill?

"I don't need twenty-four-hour care. I certainly don't need to be in hospital for another three days. Stick me in a taxi and send me home. Or let me call one of my staff from the gym to come get me," he said.

She took a deep breath. Then she entered the room. Dr. Samuels stood by the bed. Jamie only had eyes for Cooper.

He was propped in a seated position, his eyes still bandaged, his hair mussed. Her heart constricted painfully in her chest. She wanted to touch him, hold him so badly.

She hovered at the end of the bed, her hands gripping each other.

"Hi," she said. "How are you feeling?"

Cooper turned toward her.

"Jamie," he said.

Emotion swelled at the back of her throat at the relief in his voice.

She spoke in a rush, wanting to get the moment of confession over and done with.

"I brought you some things. And I've organized a nurse for you. Dr. Samuels said you'd probably be able to go home today if you had care on hand."

Cooper didn't appear to register the presumption in what she'd done. He simply turned to Dr. Samuels, satisfaction evident in every line of his body.

"See? I'll be fine," he said. "Write me up some painkillers and I'm out of here."

Dr. Samuels took a moment to review the chart in his hands before answering.

"Someone will have to apply your eyedrops in a darkened room four times a day. And I want to see you back here the day after tomorrow when the bandages can come off permanently," he instructed.

"The nurse is coming this afternoon," Jamie said. "There will be someone to look after him all the time."

Dr. Samuels nodded. "It looks like I'm releasing you into Jamie's care, Cooper."

Jamie flushed at the assumption inherent in his words.

Cooper turned his head toward her again. With his eyes bandaged, it was impossible to read his expression.

"I appreciate this," he said.

The words were too formal, too stiff for all that had passed between them.

Did he blame her? If his sight was permanently affected, would he put it down to her stupidity in being drunk and proud and pissy and not walking away from Liana's juvenile baiting?

"I'll go write up your prescriptions," the doctor said. His white coat billowed behind him as he exited.

There was a long beat of silence once they were alone.

"Just so you know, Vandenburg's been charged with assault," she said. "The Dubbo police said they'd be in contact to get a statement from you, but based on what the bartender said and other eyewitness reports, it looks like they've got a pretty good case against him."

"The doc said he hit me with a bit of pipe?"

"An old metal sign post." She shivered as she again remembered the sound of it connecting with his skull.

"Always was a gutless pussy." Cooper pushed the bedcovers back. His hospital gown was bunched up around his crotch. She swallowed at the sight of his strong thighs and calves.

"You want to pass me some clothes?" he asked as he swung his legs over the side of the bed.

She shut her mouth with a click and jumped to action.

"Right. Um, I brought you some workout pants, some underwear, a T-shirt…"

She passed each item over and watched as he located the backs of the garments by identifying clothing labels by touch.

As though he could sense her scrutiny, he gave her a half smile, his head turning toward her again. "Been here, done this before."

"Right. Of course," she said.

She wondered how long he'd lost his sight for the last time. And if having been blind before made it more or less terrifying this time around.

She felt compelled to look away when he stood and tugged his boxer briefs up over his legs. It seemed wrong to feel the pull of sexual attraction when he was so vulnerable.

"What about shoes?" he asked as he tugged the workout pants on.

"I brought your flip-flops. Thought they would be easier," she said.

"They probably won't let me walk out, anyway," he said.

She pulled his shoes from the bag and knelt at his feet. Wrapping her hand around first one ankle and then the other, she guided his feet into the sandals.

When she stood to move away, his hand shot out and grabbed her elbow, his fingers sliding down her forearm until he held her hand in his.

"Are you okay?" he asked.

His hand was warm and firm around hers. She fought the urge to twine her fingers through his and cling to him.

"Ugly enough to scare children, but the doc says it'll heal okay."

His thumb caressed the back of her hand. He opened his mouth to speak as Dr. Samuels pushed a wheelchair into the room. "Okay, I need a few signatures and then you're free to go."

Jamie slid her hand free. The doctor handed over Cooper's prescriptions and gave instructions for the application of his eyedrops, how often Cooper could have pain relief, and warning signs to look out for that would require an immediate return to hospital. Cooper signed the requisite forms, and the doctor helped settle him into the wheelchair.

She slung Cooper's overnight bag over her shoulder, then stepped into place behind the chair.

"Home, James," Cooper said in a stupid English accent.

Despite the heavy emotions weighing her down, Jamie laughed.

On the ground floor, she left him waiting in the foyer while she ran to get the car.

"I've been using your car, I hope you don't mind," she said as she guided him out the hospital doors and toward the open passenger door.

"Good. I wasn't sure how you and Arthur got back to town, and I was wondering if I'd have to send someone to Dubbo to pick it up."

"Well, you don't," she said. She leaned across him to slot his seat belt in place. He smelled of antiseptic and fresh laundry. Once again she had the overwhelming urge to press her face into him and cling like a limpet.

The car was thick with silence as she pulled away from the hospital. It was a Monday, and traffic was dense in the heart of the city. Jamie concentrated on driving his still-unfamiliar car until they'd turned off the main roads.

"Are you in any pain? Would you like to stop for anything before we go home?" she asked.

"A shower is at the top of my list, and my toothbrush," he said with a grimace. "Bed baths are just not the same as the real thing."

A stab of jealousy ripped through her as she imagined a nurse washing his big body.

Mine, her instincts screamed. *How dare you know him the way I do?*

She frowned. Her possessiveness was totally inappropriate, to say the least. She and Cooper had only had sex a handful of times. He'd indicated he wanted to see if there was something more between them, but that could mean anything. Meanwhile, she'd exploded from absolute denial of her feelings for him to…what? What was it exactly that she was feeling?

Following Cooper's instructions, she pulled into the laneway at the back of his property and discovered a hidden garage. Parking the car beside his Ferrari, she shut off the engine.

"Let's get you into the shower," she said. She winced at the forced brightness of her tone. It only highlighted how awkward she was feeling.

He got out of the car under his own steam, sliding his hand along the hood of the car until he'd walked as far as he could unguided. She stood back and let him do it on his own, understanding that he needed to do as much as he could for himself.

"If you come and stand in front of me, I can put my hand on your shoulder," he said. "That seemed to work okay for me last time."

"Of course," she said. She moved quickly to comply.

His hand was heavy and warm on her shoulder as she wove her way up the path of his artfully landscaped backyard.

"There's a step ahead," she instructed as they neared the terrace outside the back door.

"Thanks."

"We're at the back door now," she said. Her hands were shaking as she unlocked the door.

She hated seeing him like this.

Silently they moved through the house. Cooper dropped his hand from her shoulder once they'd reached the staircase. She waited at the top as he slowly ascended to join her.

"If you can adjust the showerhead so this bandage doesn't get wet and leave me a towel, I can probably handle the shower myself," he said.

She nodded, then realized he couldn't see her.

"No problem." Her voice cracked on the last word. She swallowed a lump of emotion.

She did as he asked, angling the shower arm down so that the water would spray onto his body and not onto his face, and leaving a bath sheet on the vanity.

He thanked her before turning his back and beginning to shuck his clothes.

She closed her eyes when she saw the bruises on his back and chest, the grazes on his arms from falling on the asphalt. They were no different from her own injuries, but seeing them on him was deeply disturbing and unsettling.

Was this how he'd felt when he'd seen her fight? Had he experienced the same sick feeling she had in her gut right now as she cataloged his hurts?

The rush of the shower turning on reminded her that she was once again invading Cooper's privacy. She backed out of the bathroom and waited in the hallway until she heard the water shut off.

After a few minutes of silence, he opened the door.

"I can't find my toothbrush," he said.

He was unashamedly naked and damp. She averted her eyes as she brushed past him and found what he was looking for in the vanity cabinet. Five minutes later, the bathroom door opened again and he stepped out into the hall.

He was naked still, his body dry now.

"Um, I changed your sheets and picked up a few groceries if you're hungry. I hope you don't mind…." she explained as he used the wall to guide himself to his bedroom.

He hesitated for a beat as he registered her words. Then he shuffled forward, swearing lightly when his shins connected with the frame of his bed.

She crossed to draw the curtains shut as he pulled back the covers and slid between the sheets.

"That's better," he said as he lay back against his pillows. "Now, come here."

He patted the bed. She stared at him.

"You're probably tired."

"Get your heinie over here or I'll come looking for you."

Rounding the bed, she sank reluctantly onto the mattress beside him. He reached blindly for her. One hand found her belly, the other her shoulder. She resisted as he tried to pull her closer.

"I want to make sure you're not lying to me," he said.

She stopped resisting and he slid both hands up to cup her face. He used the pads of his thumbs to survey her features with infinite tenderness, assessing her swollen lip, tracing the cut on her nose, mapping the puffiness around her eye.

"Sweetheart," he said, his voice deep with regret. "Sweet Jamie."

His touch was so gentle, his concern for her so evident. Wet heat burned at the back of her eyes. The first tear slid hotly onto her cheek and splashed onto his chest.

"Jamie," he said softly again, then he tugged her closer so that he could kiss her.

It was her undoing. Before she knew it, tears were shuddering out of her and he'd pulled her down beside him on the bed to hold her tight.

"I was so w-worried about you," she sobbed brokenly, her arms sliding around his torso to hold him tight. "When he h-hit you, I thought you were d-dead. I'm so sorry. So sorry…"

She cried her eyes out. His hands soothed her back again and again until the tide of emotion at last subsided. Slowly she became aware that her wet cheek was pressed into his bare chest, and that far from her looking after him, he was the one comforting her.

She tried to pull away, but he wouldn't let her go.

"You know, I've done a lot of crazy shit in my time," he said, holding her firmly. "But I have never in my life been so scared as when I saw you fighting that blond bitch."

He smoothed a hand over her hair. She closed her eyes and listened to his heart thumping strongly beneath her ear.

"I wasn't looking for it. I wasn't even sure I believed in it, to be honest. But I love you, Jamie," he said quietly. "I love you with everything I've got and everything that's in me."

Her breath caught in her throat. Tears pressed at the back of her eyes again. Cooper Fitzgerald loved her. Even though she'd convinced herself for a long, long time that love was the last thing she wanted in her life, she was filled with a fierce gladness that they'd found each other.

"I feel the same way," she said, pressing her face closer to his chest. She inhaled the clean male scent of him, hope rising like a bubble inside her as she allowed his words to sink in.

Cooper's chest began to vibrate. He was laughing. She lifted her head to look at him, forgetting he couldn't meet her eyes.

"What's so funny?"

"You're going to have to do better than that, sweetheart. I want to hear you say it. I *need* to hear you say it," he said. All traces of humor faded from his face as he slid his hands into her hair and caressed the nape of her neck.

"I know you've been fighting a long time, baby. I know it's been tough and dirty. But you don't need to fight against me," he said quietly. "I want you to trust me. I want you to feel safe with me. I love you."

His words hit her in the chest.

"I love you," she said. "Of course I love you."

The words came from a place deep inside, a part of herself that she'd held clenched into a fist for a very long time. Once she'd opened that fist, the words just kept tumbling out, unstoppable, raw, revealing.

"I love you so much it hurts. I love everything about you—your body, the way you look at me, the way you deal with the world, your honesty, your gentleness, your strength. I love the way you smell, and the little creases you get at the corners of your eyes just before you smile, and the way you always push your hair off your forehead when you're frustrated. I love that you can't stand it when the guys swear in front of me at the gym, and that when you look at me I can feel it in my blood and my bones. I love that you didn't hesitate to try to protect me, that you've tried to protect me from the very first moment we met, I love—"

Cooper cut off the rest of her declaration with a kiss. His tongue mated with hers as he rolled his body on top of hers, his weight pressing her down into the mattress.

Despite the fact that he'd barely been out of hospital an hour, he had no trouble finding the hem of her skirt and pushing it up toward her waist. With one flick of his wrist he had her panties down. Then he was sliding inside her, big and thick and hard.

"Say it again. All of it," he said against her neck as he began to stroke into her.

He felt so good. They felt so good. She'd been so afraid of feeling this way again. So scared of making herself weak and vulnerable. Deep inside, there was still fear, doubt, uncertainty. She'd learned wariness too well for it to dissolve so easily.

But she'd let this big, beautiful man into her life, just as she'd allowed him to join with her body. And for the moment, there wasn't a single regret in her heart.

Closing her eyes, her arms wrapped around his shoulders, she whispered her love into his ear as he drove them both a little bit crazy.

11

COOPER STIRRED to wakefulness. The first thing he registered was the warm silk of Jamie's body pressed against his, then the scent of her shampoo, and lastly the sound of her breathing, deep and steady in his ear.

He smiled as he remembered her heartfelt words, burrowing his face closer to the nape of her neck and inhaling the scent of jasmine and Jamie.

He loved her. The most stubborn, brave, prickly, sassy woman alive. He was almost grateful for Vandenburg's brutality in attacking him. Would Jamie ever have admitted her feelings if they hadn't both had the scare of a lifetime?

She shifted in bed beside him and her bare butt pressed more firmly into his groin. His cock hardened. Despite the fact that his eye was stinging and his head throbbing. Despite the fact that they'd made love barely an hour ago.

Made love.

He pressed a kiss against her shoulder and pulled her closer.

He'd had a lot of sex in his lifetime. Some good, some average, some sleazy. It had always been intense and fiery with Jamie. But touching her, being inside her, having her touch him when he knew they had a future, that she loved him and he loved her had been a revelation. Never had he felt so tender and connected, as though he would never be alone again, no matter where she was in the world. They *knew* each other, and despite them both having more than their fair share of flaws, they loved each other. After years of standing with his back to the wall, letting the world know he didn't need anyone or anything, he'd finally come home.

Jamie moved again, twisting in his arms this time and pressing a kiss to his neck.

"How are you?" she asked. Her voice was husky from sleep. "Do you need painkillers? Are you hungry?"

He opened his mouth to answer. His belly beat him to it, growling with emptiness.

"Okay, that's a yes." She laughed. "I'm not much of a cook, but I make a mean cheese on toast. It's a family specialty. I could bring it up to you in bed?"

He pulled a face. "And get toast crumbs on your nice clean sheets?"

"Ah," she said, as though she'd just discovered something new about him. It was amazing how much more nuance he could detect in her voice without his eyesight to distract him.

"Not a bed eater, then," she said.

"There are certain things I'm more than happy to eat in bed."

She laughed again, the sound low and sexy. "Hold that thought."

She rolled away from him. He felt the loss of her body heat keenly.

"I'll come down with you," he said, throwing back the covers.

He could lie and tell himself it was because he would be bored, lying in bed waiting for her to come back upstairs. The simple truth was that he wanted to be with her. After all the weeks of not being able to touch her and hold her, he suddenly had permission. He wasn't even close to having his fill of her yet.

She passed him his robe, and he heard the rustle of clothing as she dressed.

"What are you wearing?" he asked. He wanted to picture her in his mind's eye.

"A black skirt and a red T-shirt," she said.

"Is the T-shirt tight?"

"Tight enough."

"Tell me you didn't put your bra and panties back on," he said.

"I didn't."

He made an appreciative noise. She came and took him by the hand.

"Food first," she said. "I'm supposed to be looking after you, not riding you like a pony at the fair."

"But if the pony wants to be ridden…"

She led him toward the door. "Stop tempting me. You know I have no self-control where you're concerned."

He filed that little piece of information away as she guided him to the top of the stairs and placed his hand on the banister. He liked that she didn't try to cosset him and that she understood he needed and wanted to do as much for himself as possible. She hadn't tried to dress him at the hospital or insisted on supervising him in the shower. She understood. But on an instinctive level, they'd always understood each other, hadn't they?

He could hear her feet on the floorboards ahead of him as he descended the stairs. He followed her to the kitchen, one hand on the wall. He didn't have a lot of decorative crap in his house, so he could move freely, knowing there were no vases to knock over or hall tables to walk into. One hand extended in front of himself, he found the edge of the island counter in the kitchen and walked along it until he bumped into the first of the three stools tucked beneath it.

He sat, resting his elbows on the cool granite counter.

"The light's flashing on your answering machine. Do you want to check your messages?" she asked.

"Sure."

There was a click, then the stilted voice of a man who was very aware he was talking to a machine.

"This is the Dubbo police calling for Cooper Fitzgerald. Mr. Fitzgerald, we need to interview you regarding the assault charges we have laid against Kyle Vandenburg relating to the incident on Saturday, December twelfth. Please call us to let us know when it would be suitable for an officer to attend your house to take your statement."

The policeman reeled off a number, then the machine beeped to indicate there were more messages.

"This is Alice Jenkins from the *Daily Telegraph* calling. Mr. Fitzgerald, I'd love to talk to you about your recent experience in Dubbo. If you could call me as soon as you get this message, that would be—"

The machine cut off before the message finished and Cooper guessed Jamie had deleted it. There were three more messages after that one, all of them reporters. They all got the same treatment—a few seconds of air time, then deletion.

"I'm a popular guy," he said.

"Bloody parasites."

He could hear the sounds of her working in the kitchen, and he tried to identify each noise. The *click-squelch* of the fridge opening and shutting, the rustle of a plastic bread bag, the slide of containers being placed on the counter.

"My mother used to make me cheese on toast when I was a kid," he said.

It was the one thing he'd always been certain of growing up—no matter how out of it his mom was, there would always be a loaf of white bread in the pantry and a pack of processed cheese slices in the fridge. In her messed-up, half-assed way, she'd tried to do her best for him.

There was a long pause before Jamie asked him if he wanted tomato on his toast or not. He didn't need to see her face to know that she'd wanted to ask him more. She was so careful with her own privacy, he knew she would never push.

He waited until they were seated on the couch, a plate each on their knees before he spoke up.

"It's okay, you know. If you want to ask questions."

He heard the rustle of clothes as she shifted beside him.

"What happened that you had to leave home?" she asked quietly.

He swallowed a mouthful before he answered.

"My mother was a heroin addict. She did the best she could, but she had lousy taste in men. Most of them weren't particularly happy to have a little kid hanging around."

There was a small silence as Jamie digested what he'd told her and he ate his toast.

"Did they hit you?"

"Yeah. Some of them worse than others. And they hit her, too. It was bloody miserable."

His fingers tightened on the plate as he had a sudden flash of memory: his mother curled into a ball, trying to protect herself, him throwing himself into the fray, trying to save her. He'd felt so helpless, so damned powerless....

That quickly he understood why it had been so hard for him to watch Jamie get hurt in the ring. Watching her under attack tapped into some deep shit for him.

He was still examining the realization when Jamie spoke up again.

"I bet you wish you could go back in time and beat the living crap out of some of them. What kind of coward beats up on women and little kids?" Her voice vibrated with anger.

"I did run into one of them once. Just after I started winning my first few fights. Guy actually had the balls to come up to me after the bout and ask if I remembered him. Like that was a good thing and I'd be happy to see him again." He shook his head at the memory.

"What did you do?" she asked.

"I wanted to hit him, but I was nearly a foot taller than him and twice as wide. I walked away. You can let that stuff own you, or you can use it to get what you want in life. I won't ever forget where I came from, but it's not the most important part of me."

It was important she understand that. He was a lot more than a kid who'd had a hard time growing up. His demons didn't ride him anymore.

He wished he could see her face but had to be satisfied with reaching across to touch her thigh.

"Is your mother still alive?" she asked. Her hand pressed down on his.

"No. She OD'd when I was twenty."

Another small silence. Then Jamie cleared her throat.

"My mom died when I was eighteen. Cancer. I thought she was too young at the time, but later I was glad she wasn't around to see what Jack did to us. She used to be so proud of him, his number-one fan."

Jamie often referred to her father by name. It was something he'd noticed before. As though she was trying to distance herself from him, deny his role in her life. His gut told him that they must have been very close. The deeper the connection, the more bitter the betrayal, in his experience. And Jamie was very bitter and angry when it came to her father.

"Your old man was a hero to me when I was coming up through the ranks," he said. "He had so much heart and tenacity. I used to watch his fights over and over to psych myself up sometimes."

Jamie stiffened, then slid her hand away from his. "What do you think is going to happen to Vandenburg?" she asked. "Do you think he'll be banned from boxing if he's found guilty?"

There was a beat of silence as he processed the change of subject. They weren't going to talk about Jack Sawyer.

No surprises there.

"They might suspend him for a while, but I doubt he'll be banned. Tyson fought again after he did jail time, remember?"

She took his plate from his lap and he heard her move back into the kitchen. He pushed away a flicker of concern over her refusal to discuss her father. Talking wasn't the only way to deal with things. He'd walked away from enough heavy conversations in his lifetime. He'd like for her to talk to him, to let him in fully, but there was no rush. Today, it was enough that she loved him. Anything else was bonus material.

JAMIE STACKED the lunch dishes in the dishwasher, very aware of the silence in the room after she'd diverted their conversation into less personal channels. She opened her mouth to try to explain to Cooper about her father. The only words that came to mind were so angry that she swallowed them again. She didn't want to taint this special time with Cooper with her father's legacy. It wouldn't do any good, and it wouldn't change anything. Maybe, one day, she would tell him. When the knot of anger and guilt inside her wasn't so tight and complicated.

The nurse came at four. They survived three whole hours with her in the house before Jamie had a hurried consultation with Cooper and sent her home.

She didn't want someone else looking after him. She wanted to do it herself. Old-fashioned, but it was how she felt, what instinct demanded. She was his lover. Quite literally, the woman who loved him. And it seemed only right that she express that love by looking after him when he was injured and living with the prospect of losing the sight in his left eye.

She phoned into work to let them know she was taking all the sick days she had owing—four in total. Her boss wasn't happy, and Jamie wondered if she'd have a job to go back to. It didn't matter. Cooper was more important than cleaning bathtubs and using maid origami on the toilet roll. Anyway, she had two purses under her belt now, and though most of this weekend's prize money would be chewed up by the lingering bills from having her car fixed, she'd have enough left to keep the wolf from the door for a few weeks if she had to find another job.

That night after dinner, she dimmed the lights in Cooper's bedroom and applied his eyedrops. She cradled his head in her lap, holding his strong jaw. She felt swamped by tenderness. He was so strong, but also so fragile. He'd had a horrible childhood, but he'd survived it to claw his way to the top of his chosen field. He'd literally conquered the world—just as he'd conquered her.

Reapplying his bandage, she kissed his forehead and smoothed his hair back.

"Are you tired?" she asked.

"A little. Why, what have you got in mind?" he asked. She heard the underlying desire in his voice and understood the question he was asking. She craved him again, too.

Would it always be this way between them? Sometimes it felt as though they'd barely rolled away from each other before need was building between them again.

She studied him, her gaze skimming his body.

"Why don't you just relax," she said.

He smiled slowly. "I think I can handle that."

He lifted his head so she could slide out from beneath him. Stretching alongside him on the bed, she smoothed her hands down the satin of his bathrobe. She undid the sash slowly, and pushed the robe off his shoulders. He had such a beautiful body. She saw with a surge of desire that he was already hard for her, his cock a rigid demand against his belly.

She could feel herself getting wet just looking at him. She licked her lips. She wanted him inside her again very badly. But first she wanted to taste him and drive him a little bit crazy, the way he'd driven her crazy that night before her fight.

Trailing her hands through the hair on his chest, she followed the narrowing arrow down, down into the thick, dark curls surrounding his erection.

She wrapped her palm around him, sliding her hand up and down his shaft a few times. She watched as his mouth parted a fraction and his jaw muscles tightened. Enjoying her power, she wriggled farther down the bed and took him in her mouth.

He tasted clean and hot, and he was very, very hard. She traced the head of his cock with her tongue, then flicked him again and again while working his shaft with her hand. He lifted his hips and made an encouraging noise as she took him all the way into her mouth, marveling at his length and breadth. He groaned. She could feel his belly muscles tensing as his desire built. Using her mouth and her hand in concert, she began to work him, laving the head of his cock with the flat of her tongue, then flicking it, then sucking him deep into her mouth.

"Shift up the bed," he said. "I want to touch you."

She obliged, angling her legs toward him even as she continued to suck and lick him. He found her knees by touch and pushed them apart. He slid a hand past her skirt and up her thigh. She swallowed a moan as his fingers found her folds, gliding into her slick wetness.

"Oh, man," he muttered. She felt his body tense even more as he began to explore her with deft fingers, delving between her legs to plunge a finger inside her, then sliding out again to circle and tease and torture her clit.

She tortured him in turn, stepping up the rhythm as she responded to the increasing urgency gripping her own body.

She loved the way his whole body was focused on what she was doing to him and what he was doing to her. Closing her eyes, she felt her orgasm rising.

Her desire fed his, and he sucked in a breath, his body tensing as he came. Savouring his salty sweetness, she gasped as her own climax took her at last, crashing down on her and sweeping her away.

She rested her head on his thigh for a few beats afterward, her whole body warm and liquid.

"Take your clothes off," he said. She lifted her head to look at him. His cheeks were flushed. She knew that if she could see his eyes they'd be dark and smoky with passion. In front of her, his cock stirred to life again.

An answering throb pulsed between her thighs.

Unbelievable.

She pulled her clothes off, then slid up his body, enjoying the subtle friction of his hairy chest against her breasts.

She found his mouth and kissed him hungrily, pressing herself against his hardness.

"I can't get enough of you," he whispered into her mouth.

"I feel the same way," she said.

His belly tensed beneath her as he huffed out a surprised laugh at her echoing of her earlier comment.

While he was distracted, she grabbed his cock, positioned herself above him and slid home.

"Jamie," he said as she embraced him in her slick heat.

"Yes." She knew exactly what he was feeling and didn't have the words to say.

Pleasure that was so intense it was almost pain. *Desire* that was so demanding it felt as though it could never be sated. *Need* that was so overwhelming, she had no hope of ever denying it.

Bracing her hands on either side of his head, she started to ride up and down his thick shaft, circling her hips as she sought the friction and rhythm they both needed. She lowered her head and kissed him. Her tongue plunged deeply into his mouth, and his rose up to meet it. Her nipples brushed back and forth across his chest, stiff with arousal.

Inevitably desire built again. She broke their kiss to concentrate on where they were joined, her hips flexing and releasing. Her breath came in gasps as she closed her eyes and chased glory.

"I wish I could see you," Cooper groaned, his hands sliding up her rib cage to find her breasts, his fingers teasing her nipples.

"Next time," she panted. "And the time after that."

As if the thought of all the *next times* they would have

spurred him on, Cooper's head dropped back. His fingers tensed around her waist as he pumped up into her once, twice, three times. She opened her eyes to watch his orgasm take him, infinitely turned on by way his whole body arched and his lips pulled back from his teeth in an animal snarl.

Then it was her turn to die a little. She slid down his shaft one last time and felt her body shatter around him, heat and sensation pulsing through her until she was left limp and gasping.

Flopping down onto his chest, she pressed kisses into the curve of his neck.

"I love you," she gasped. "I love you so much."

He withdrew from her and rolled her to one side so he could pull her tight against the cradle of his body. She lay in the shelter of his arms as her breathing slowed, her mind adrift in a formless ocean of sensation and tiredness and gratitude and satisfaction.

"I think you should move in," Cooper said as their heartbeats returned to normal.

She stiffened instinctively. *Move in?* As in, live with him? In each other's pockets day in, day out? In the same bed, night after night?

"I live with my grandfather," she said.

"This is a four-bedroom house," he said. "Next objection?"

She frowned as she thought furiously.

"I have no more objections," she admitted after a small silence.

He stilled, then kissed her deeply. His hands slid into her hair as he drank from her lips.

"Give me half an hour and we'll celebrate properly," he promised.

WAKING IN Cooper's arms the next morning only confirmed Jamie's decision. She loved him. She wanted to be with him. She was still afraid, still cautious about exposing herself, of being vulnerable. But the love and desire she felt for him far out-weighed her fear.

Her grandfather greeted the news with a sniff when she called him before lunch and told him.

"In my day, we married before we lived together," he said.

"When was your day again, Grandpa?" she teased lightly. "Before or after the dinosaurs?"

He spluttered out a laugh at her cheekiness, then was suddenly serious.

"You sound happy, Jimmy. Is this really what you want?"

"I love him," she said simply. "And he loves me. We want to be together."

Her grandfather cleared his throat. "Well. You tell Cooper I'll stop polishing my shotgun after what I saw the other night, then."

"He'll be relieved, I know," Jamie said with a smile. She shot a look to where Cooper was eating a bowl of cereal at the kitchen counter.

"I've had a couple of phone calls for you while you were gone. The international news services must have picked up on your fight because one of them was American."

"Yeah? Huh," Jamie said, frowning.

"You want me to give them Cooper's number if they call again?"

"Sure. Why not?" She might hate the press, but building a reputation for herself in the States would be good for her career.

She spent the rest of the day lounging around the house with Cooper. They did a crossword, then she succumbed to Cooper's cajoling and finally read him the newspaper's version of what had happened in Dubbo. They had two days' worth of newsprint to pick over by then. Sunday's paper was full of her win and the surprise revelation of her identity, and she skimmed over the story quickly, not wanting to dwell on the background material they'd dug up about her father. Jack's fraud convic-tion and suicide two years ago were the stuff of journalists' wet dreams, and she refused to read yet more column inches on a subject that had already caused her enough pain. Monday's paper was focused more on the fight in the parking lot, going over Vandenburg's fight history and briefly recapping the two professional bouts the two men had had in the ring. Cooper smiled broadly as she read him the journalist's assessment that Vandenburg had resorted to "dirty tricks and thuggery" when it became clear that Cooper had beaten him yet again.

"They're pushing pretty hard," Cooper concluded. "Maybe he will get suspended."

"Couldn't happen to a better asshole," she said.

A police officer from the local precinct came by in the early afternoon to take Cooper's statement on behalf of the Dubbo police, and toward the end of the afternoon, she took him for a drive, just to get out of the house.

They wound up in bed after an early dinner. It was where they both wanted to be—where their hormones and emotions demanded they be.

Afterward, she lay with her head on his chest and a hand on his belly.

"Your doctor's appointment is tomorrow," she said after a long silence.

"Yep."

She knew from conversations they'd had after she'd applied his eyedrops that he could discern light through his injured eye. A positive sign, Cooper said.

"Are you worried?" she asked. She was. He'd have to be superhuman not to be.

"There are a bunch of people who get by without any sight at all," he said. "Even if the news is bad, I'll deal with it. But I don't think it will be. It feels good. Itchy as all hell, but good."

The doctor agreed with his self-assessment the next day. While Jamie clutched Cooper's hand, Dr. Samuels eased the pad off and examined his eye.

It was red and sore-looking, but Cooper quickly confirmed that he could see.

It took Jamie a moment to realize she was crying.

"I don't know what's wrong with me," she told Cooper, sniffing the tears away. "I swear, before I met you I hadn't cried for years."

"My special gift to you," Cooper said.

With a checkup scheduled for the following week, they drove home again. Cooper was quiet. She kept shooting glances at him as she drove. Sensing her scrutiny, he met her gaze and silently reassured her by taking her hand in his and smiling. Happiness washed over her. He was going to be okay.

Cooper's mind had turned to gym business by the time they pulled into the garage at his place. He was listing the calls he needed to make when they reentered the house. Absently he pressed the flashing light on the answering machine to retrieve his messages, and they both froze when they heard an American accent boom out into the room.

"This is Lewis White calling from the U.S. I'm looking for Jamie Sawyer. Jamie, if you want to call me back, I've got an offer to put to you."

The caller reeled off a long number.

Cooper swore and reached for the delete button. Jamie caught his finger just in time.

"What are you doing? Lewis White is one of the biggest fight promoters in the U.S.," she said. As though he didn't know that already.

"He's a lying, sneaky piece of crap," Cooper said. "If he wants to offer you something, wait until we've found you another trainer."

"I should at least speak to him, see what he's offering."

"No," Cooper said, shaking his head. "Fighters who deal directly with promoters get done over. Trust me, I've seen it happen too many times to count."

She frowned. "So I just don't respond? What could it hurt to talk to the guy?"

"If you want to get a start on the U.S. circuit, leave it up to someone who knows to steer you right."

Jamie bit her lip. The need to find another trainer was but one of many things that she'd shoved to one side while Cooper recovered. How long would it take before she had someone else lined up? And what would happen to the deal Lewis White was offering in the meantime?

"I'm going to call him back," she said.

Cooper's jaw tensed, but he didn't say another word. He stood with arms crossed over his chest while she listened to the message again, jotting down the phone number before pulling out her cell phone.

Lewis White answered on the third ring.

"Mr. White. My name is Jamie Sawyer. You left a message for me," she explained, very aware of Cooper hovering darkly at her elbow.

"I've been trying to get a hold of you for two days now. You're a tough lady to track down," Lewis White said.

"Sorry about that, I've been busy."

"Ms. Sawyer, I'm going to cut to the chase since I'm in a bit of a time jam here. You ever heard of a fighter called Roma Williams?"

Jamie's pulse quickened.

"Of course I have. She's the world number five," she said. She'd seen Roma fight a half dozen times at Ray's place on cable. She was scary good.

"I've got a fight scheduled between Williams and an up-and-coming Philly girl by the name of Larissa Farnam in Las Vegas in six weeks' time—ten rounds, a half-million-dollar purse. Problem is Ms. Farnam has gone and broken her leg in a training accident."

"Right," Jamie said.

"Which leaves me looking for a replacement. I won't lie to you—you weren't my first or even second choice. But I heard about what you did to Liana Nelson on the weekend and people who know say that you can fight. I figure we might get as many folks interested in seeing Jack Sawyer's little girl strut her stuff in the ring as Ms. Farnam. So, are you interested?"

Jamie blinked. Her head was spinning.

Roma Williams.

She was being offered a shot at the world number five. If she won, it would fast-track her career and put her that much closer to a title fight.

"You still there, Ms. Sawyer?" Lewis asked, his American accent echoing down the line.

"Yes. I'm still here. And yes, I'll take it," she said.

Cooper's eyebrows snapped together in a frown.

"What? What are you taking?"

She gave Lewis White her e-mail address so he could send through the pertinent details. Cooper put a hand on her shoulder.

"Let me talk to him," he said, holding out a hand.

"I'll speak to you soon, Mr. White," Jamie said, ending the call before Cooper could snatch the phone from her hand.

"What did you just agree to?" Cooper asked.

"I'm fighting Roma Williams in Las Vegas in six weeks' time." She said it defiantly, challengingly, because she knew that Cooper was going to object. He flushed a dull red and thumped a hand down onto the kitchen counter.

"What the hell, Jamie," he said. "Have you seen your face? That eye alone is going to take three weeks to heal. And you want to go into the ring in six? You've just taken a major pounding."

"I'll be fine. I'm a fast healer."

"Roma Williams is a tough fighter."

She crossed her arms over her chest. "And?"

"She's much more experienced than you. You're not ready for her."

His words stung. A lot.

"Really? Thanks for the vote of confidence. I'll try to keep those inspirational words in mind when I'm in the ring."

"You've had three fights, Jamie. This woman is a seasoned pro. You're not ready."

"I want this fight. And I'm going to win it," she said, setting her jaw stubbornly.

He swore. "Jamie…"

"You're not my trainer anymore. You don't have a say in this stuff," she said.

He stared at her. "This is not about who is or isn't your trainer. Anyone you take on is going to say the same thing—wait. Build yourself up. Get more fights under your belt. Then take on the big girls."

"If I win this, I'll be only a few fights away from a title shot."

"And if you lose your debut on the U.S. scene will be a defeat. What do you think that'll do to your chances?"

Anger made her body stiff. "I'm willing to take the risk."

She turned away from him, started walking up the hallway.

"This discussion is not over," he said, his words following her.

She climbed the stairs and collected the few personal items she'd brought with her. Cooper watched from the hallway as she descended again and headed for the front door.

"What are you doing?"

"I'm going home to where people believe in me," she said.

"I believe in you, Jamie. I believe in you so much I want you to have a long, successful career, not some publicity-driven freak show."

Her mouth fell open. "*Freak show?* Thanks a lot."

"That's what this is. Using your name to get a bunch of morons to gawk at Jack Sawyer's daughter. Lewis White'll be hammering the publicity, your dad's name will be everywhere. None of it will be about you."

She eyed him steadily. "It isn't about me, anyway. This is

about my grandfather redeeming his name. I thought you understood that."

Her back stiff, she left the house.

If Cooper didn't believe in her, he could go screw himself.
She might love him, but she wasn't giving up her dreams for
him. And if he didn't understand that, then he wasn't the man
she thought he was.

12

"THIS IS A BAD fight, Jimmy."

Jamie braced one leg in front of the other and stretched out her calf muscles.

It had been four weeks since she'd spoken to Lewis White and walked out of Cooper's house. She was sick of people trying to tell her what to do. First Cooper, then her grandfather and now Ray.

"It's a fine fight, and I'm going to win," she said through her teeth.

Ray rolled his eyes toward the sky.

"Man, you're such an idiot sometimes."

"Feel free to leave, then. I'm kind of busy anyway, in case you hadn't noticed, training for a fight."

Straightening, Jamie crossed to the long bag hanging in the corner. Ray followed, his bruised face creased with concern. He'd won his second bout under Cooper's aegis two nights ago. She'd watched the fight on TV at a local sports bar, beamed live from the U.K. Cooper and Ray had landed back in Sydney this morning, she knew, but only Ray had gone to the trouble of tracking her down in her new gym. Which was fine by her. She'd had more than enough arguments with Cooper over the past four weeks. She didn't need yet more proof that the man she loved didn't believe in her.

"This place is a dive," Ray said, his expression disparaging as he scanned the dimly lit room.

Located at the end of an alleyway in the red light district of Kings Cross, Jamie's new gym smelled of old urine and damp and most of the equipment was eaten by rust. It was a far cry from Fitzgerald's, to say the least.

"No shit," she said.

"Jimmy. Think about what you're doing. Listen to the people who love you. You really think me, Cooper and Arthur have all got it wrong?"

Jamie began to pepper the long bag with combinations.

"I know what I'm doing. This is what I want." She'd said it so often lately, she was thinking of getting T-shirts made. Maybe that way people would back off and leave her alone.

Her grandfather was angry with her. Every moment she spent in the apartment with him was fraught with tension. Christmas had been an unmitigated disaster, with the two of them stiffly exchanging presents and making awkward small talk over a turkey meal at the local pub. As for Cooper…Cooper could barely stay in the same room with her for more than five minutes. Three times he'd come over and tried to talk her around, and each time they'd wound up yelling at each other. She hadn't seen him for nearly ten days now. It scared her how much she missed him.

It wasn't the sex. It was everything. She loved him. She'd been about to move in with him, her and her grandfather. Then all this crap had blown up.

She could still remember their parting words a week and a half ago.

"People get hurt in fights when they're outclassed, Jamie. People die," he'd said.

She'd stared at him, willing him to understand. "I have to do this. I need this."

"Do you want me to beg? Because I'll get down on my knees if that's what it's going to take."

It had gotten ugly from there.

Why couldn't he believe in her? Why couldn't he understand that this was something she had to do? She'd explained to him about her grandfather, about her father, and how she needed to do this for her family. Why couldn't he see that this was not negotiable? She had to take this thing as far as it would go and then some. She had to shove her fist down the world's throat and force everyone to forget the shame.

Ray leaned against the wall near the long bag, watching her pound shots into the heavy leather.

"Cooper's like a bear with a sore head without you around. He was an asshole all the way to England and back again."

"So?"

Ray adjusted the band on his watch. "Do you love him?" he asked casually.

Jamie flicked him a look. "Why? You looking for one for old times' sake?"

Ray's lips curled into a reluctant smile. "Just answer the question."

"Yes."

"Do you respect him? As a fighter? As a trainer?"

"You know I do."

"Then listen to him. He's right. Don't go to Vegas."

Jamie slammed an uppercut into the bag, channeling all the fury and frustration that had been building inside her for the past few weeks. Rounding on Ray, she took it right up to him so that they were toe-to-toe.

"I can look after myself. And I know what I want. I don't care if all of you don't think I can do it—*I am going to win.* And I'm going to keep on winning until I've got that world championship belt in my hands and my grandfather can hold his head high again."

Ray stared at her.

"Your grandfather doesn't want you to do this."

"I made a promise," she said. She turned away from him.

"What? What promise?"

"It doesn't matter. There's nothing you can say that's going to change my mind, Ray."

She started in on the long bag again.

"I heard a rumor while I was away. That you'd taken on Paul Murphy as your new trainer," Ray said after a short silence. "Tell me it was bullshit."

"Paul Murphy is a good trainer," she said as she punched the bag.

"About a hundred years ago. Now he's a second-stringer, if that, and you know it."

She didn't bother to argue. Paul was old, past his prime, and only a year or two away from retirement altogether.

"I need a trainer. I can't go to Vegas without one."

"Then take the time to find someone good. Someone who comes even remotely close to replacing Cooper."

Jamie locked her jaw and kept throwing punches. Paul Murphy gave her legitimacy in the eyes of the boxing world, and that was all she needed or wanted from him. They'd come to a tacit understanding on the subject within the first few days of working with each other. Now, he made a token effort to turn up for training a couple of times a week, and she continued to follow the routine Cooper had created for her when she was in training for the Dubbo fight.

After a few minutes of being ignored, Ray headed for the door. She slowed then stopped after he'd gone, staring blankly at the worn leather in front of her.

It would have been nice if Ray had been on her side. It was tough not having anyone in her corner. She'd never fought with her grandfather this way before. And it was even tougher dealing with Cooper's disapproval and silence.

About the only good news she'd had lately was the boxing association's decision to ban Kyle Vandenburg for three years. Given his age, it was a career-ending penalty. As she'd said to Cooper previously, it couldn't have happened to a better asshole.

Her face twisted with regret as she remembered those few golden days of nursing Cooper after his operation. It had been so hard to let him into her heart. Now she felt as though she'd made that leap of faith for nothing.

Her spine straightened. He was stubborn, just like her, but he wouldn't walk away from what they had out of pure pride.

When she won, he would see that she was right, and he would come back to her.

She had to believe that, because she couldn't deal with the alternative. Not when she was up against so much negativity already.

Taking a deep breath, she started up again. Left, right, jab, cross. Focus. Footwork. Protect herself.

Right now, that was all that mattered.

"YOU SHOULD HAVE done something. You should have stopped her."

Cooper looked up from his computer to find Arthur Sawyer in his office doorway. The old man's face was red with anger as he strode forward belligerently.

Jamie had flown to the States yesterday. Cooper had refused to give even tacit support to the fight by saying goodbye or seeing her off at the airport. He was furious with her—furious that his opinion and expertise and feelings meant so little to her, and that she'd replaced him with a trainer so past his prime it was a joke. He had no idea what had happened to the warm intimacy and honesty they'd shared after his operation. Once the fight offer was on the table, she'd simply shut down, turning back into the stubborn, closed-off, driven woman she'd been when he first met her.

He'd thought they were past that. Clearly they weren't. He had no idea what to do about any of it. The only thing he knew for sure was that he couldn't stand outside the ring and watch

Roma Williams pound Jamie into the canvas. Not again. He loved her too much to watch her suffer.

"What should I have done, Arthur? Kidnap her until after the fight? Lock her away until she saw sense?"

Arthur paced in front of the desk, his shoulders hunched. "I don't know. Something! You should have done something."

Cooper knew the old man was railing at him out of guilt because he, too, had refused to go to Vegas with Jamie, but it still pissed him off. Especially when she was putting herself on the line like this for him.

"You're the one she's doing this for. You should have released her from her promise if you were serious about stopping her," he said.

Arthur's head swung around. "What? What the hell are you talking about?"

Cooper stared at the other man.

"What promise? Tell me," Arthur demanded.

"You don't know anything about it, do you?" Cooper said, realization slowly dawning.

"What promise?" Arthur repeated, drawing himself to his full height, his voice low and menacing.

"Jamie told me she made a promise to you when you were sick in hospital after your heart attack. To redeem the family name and make things right for you. She seemed to think you were ashamed, that you'd lost your standing with your buddies and had nothing to live for."

Arthur swore, his face mottled red with emotion.

"I always assumed you knew," Cooper said.

"Well, I didn't. You think I want my granddaughter to get busted up in that ring? When she told me she wanted to take up boxing, I was dead set against it. She's such a beautiful girl. Before all the mess with Jack and Vandenburg she was so happy and joyful. Hell, she was training to be a naturopath, can you believe it? She was going to be a healer, not a bruiser. But she was so damned determined, and I saw it meant a lot to her so I supported her, did my best by her." The old man's voice quavered.

Cooper stood and went to his side.

"Listen. It's not your fault. Jamie thought you were going to die. She thinks she's giving you your pride back."

Arthur sank into a chair and put his head into his hands.

"This is about Jack," he said after a long beat. "In my heart I always knew it was, but I could never make myself bring it up. I knew I should have made her talk to someone after we found him. She was so quiet afterward, it was unnatural. No tears, nothing."

Cooper stilled. "Jamie told me *you* found his body."

"We both did. He…Jack did it in the garage of the apartment we were renting. I walked in first, then Jimmy. She was the one who cut him down…."

Cooper closed his eyes.

Poor Jamie.

No wonder she was so angry at the world. No wonder she felt so betrayed.

"Until he threw that fight, she idolized him so bad," Arthur said, his eyes vacant as he stared straight ahead. "Never seen anything like it—right from when she was born she was daddy's little girl. She watched him train, she came to every fight, trailed around after him like a shadow. As far as she was concerned, he could do no wrong. Then he threw that fight."

Arthur let his breath out with a loud, defeated sigh.

"Don't know why he did it. He'd always liked splashing out on fancy cars and whatnot. He had money, but maybe he was worried it wouldn't be enough with no more purses coming in. God knows, there are enough stories of ex-champs living on welfare to scare a retired fighter. I figured he'd just gotten greedy. The truth is, he never offered to explain, and I never asked. This sport can be ugly sometimes. But Jamie… Jamie was shattered. All the press, then the trial. His boxing buddies turning their backs on him, mouthing off about him, calling him a fraud. The light went out inside her. I guess she felt like he'd been lying to her all those years, letting her think he was larger than life when really he was just a man like anyone else. When he came home from prison, she could barely look him in the eye. He broke her heart, and she broke his right back."

Cooper rubbed the bridge of his nose as the pieces fell into place. Jamie's reticence. Her anger. Her burning need for redemption.

He should have pushed her harder. He'd known she was angry with her father—he simply hadn't realized how deep and dark it all ran. He should have cracked her open and forced it out of her. But he'd thought he had all the time in the world.

Reaching for his car keys, he grabbed the old man's elbow. "Come on, let's go," he said.

"Where?"

"Where do you think?"

JAMIE DANCED FROM FOOT to foot, punching the air. Right, left, right, right, left. Behind her, the massage therapist she'd hired packed up his table. Having him work on her hadn't been anything like when Cooper had rubbed her down before her last fight, talking to her all the while, telling her how strong she was, that she was going to go out there and win. Her new trainer, Murphy, had tried to offer her pre-fight advice, but she'd sent him out of the room. The only people she wanted in her corner were thousands of miles away, and she didn't want some pale imitation mouthing platitudes to her.

She knew what she had to do. That would have to suffice.

Her hands were taped, her body warm. Soon Murphy would

return and lace her into her gloves. Already she could hear the crowd roaring outside. This was the biggest audience she'd ever fought in front of. When they cheered the walls vibrated and the corridors thundered.

She'd tried to call her grandfather before Murphy had taped her hands. He hadn't picked up. Neither had Cooper when she'd tried him.

She'd been so sure that he'd relent at the last minute. She'd grown used to him coming through for her.

More fool her.

She threw some more punches at her invisible opponent.

It didn't matter. She was about to prove both Cooper and her grandfather wrong.

And if she didn't...

She couldn't let her mind go there. She had everything riding on this fight. Financially as well as emotionally. Her boss had looked at her incredulously when she'd asked for the time off to fly to Vegas. Jamie had pushed, despite knowing that she didn't exactly have a spotless work record and that she'd fallen even further out of favor by trading off shifts lately so she could train for the big fight. Now she was officially unemployed— just in case she needed further incentive to win tonight.

A cool breeze hit her as the door behind her opened. Murphy returning to lace her gloves. She kept shadowboxing as she spoke over her shoulder.

"I'll be with you in a minute," she said.

"Jamie."

She froze, then slowly pivoted on her heel. Cooper stood there, a brown paper parcel in his hands.

"You came," she said. A smile curved her lips. She started toward him.

"To try to make you see sense one last time," he said.

Her smile died. She stopped in her tracks. "Then you can get out."

"Your grandfather is here. He doesn't want you to do this for him, Jamie. I told him about your promise, and he doesn't want you going out there in his name."

"I'm doing this for both of us," she said.

"No, you're not. You're doing this because of your father."

"I'm here to make things right," she said fiercely, her hands fisting.

"Yeah? Really?" Cooper asked. His blue eyes pierced her, nailing her to the wall. "Is that really why you want to step into the ring and take all that pain?"

Suddenly she was furious. How dare he come into her change room before a fight and challenge her like this? She needed to be focused, her mind clear, her purpose absolute.

"You say you love me, yet you're here trying to screw me up," she shouted. "You're supposed to be on my side."

"I'm here to help set you free, Jamie."

She glared at him coldly.

"Get out. And don't come back. I don't want anyone in my life who doesn't believe in me."

Cooper held her eye steadily for a long moment, then he nodded.

"I'll go. But first I want to give you this."

He held out the parcel. She eyed it warily.

"What is it?"

"Take it. Open it. Prove to me that you're here for all the right reasons," he said.

"I don't have to prove anything to you."

He threw the parcel at her. She caught it instinctively. It was heavier than she'd expected and the paper rustled beneath her hands.

"Open it."

"You're such an asshole," she said. "But if this is what it takes to get rid of you, fine."

Digging her fingers into the paper, she made a hole and tore the parcel open. Shiny blue and white satin slithered across her hands and the smell of mothballs and old sweat swamped her.

A single word arched across the fabric, white satin stitched on blue.

SAWYER.

Her father's fight robe.

She dropped the parcel as though she'd been gut-punched.

"Your father wouldn't want you to punish yourself like this," Cooper said. "He loved you. He'd hate for you to get hurt in his name."

Jamie pressed her hands to her chest, fighting hard to breathe. A heavy weight was pressing down on her, suffocating her. "I'm not doing it for him. He was a cheat, a fraud. I hate him."

"No, you don't. You love him," Cooper said quietly. "You love him more than anything in the world."

Jamie shook her head, trying to deny his words, but something dark and hidden was rising up inside her. Her gaze darted around the change room as she tried to find some way of escaping the truth, but she couldn't and suddenly she was gasping, tears streaming down her face, Cooper's strong arms closing around her.

"There was no reason for him to do what he did. No reason at all," she sobbed. "We didn't need the money. We didn't need anything. I couldn't understand. He was the best man I knew. And then he did this thing. This horrible, dishonest thing that made a lie of everything that had come before it."

"He made a mistake," Cooper said.

"I thought he was perfect. I loved him so much...."

She clung to Cooper's broad shoulders then as it all came pouring out: her father's guilt and remorse, her own sense of anger and outrage and fear that the hero she'd built all the certainties in her life around had turned out to be so incredibly ordinary and human and fallible. And lastly the final dark week when he'd been released from prison and discovered that the world of boxing was forever barred to him and his old friends had turned away and his own daughter couldn't forgive him.

"He asked me. He looked me in the eye and asked me if I would ever forget what he'd done, if I could ever think of him in the same way again. I was so angry with him still. We'd lost everything because of the court fees and because I let Kyle screw me over, and I blamed him. I wanted to hurt him. So I said nothing. The next day he killed himself."

"It wasn't your fault, Jamie."

She lifted her head, looking at him through tear-soaked eyes. "He asked for one kind word, one moment of reassurance, and I couldn't give it to him."

"*It wasn't your fault.* Your father made a decision when he decided to throw that fight, and he couldn't live with the consequences. You didn't hold a gun to his head and tell him to do it. You didn't send him to prison or harass him in the media. You didn't tell his friends to ostracize him."

"I should have told him I forgave him. I should have told him I understood, that things would get better," she said.

Cooper gripped her by the shoulders and shook her lightly. "Listen to me. Your father was a grown man. He made a choice, and it was his choice, and only his. You cannot wear this, Jamie. It's not your burden to carry. And you can't keep going into that ring and punishing yourself as some kind of penance for what you think you did. You loved your father, and he knew it. Anything else is on his shoulders."

She wanted to believe him. She wanted to set down the weight that she'd been carrying for so long. But her guilt was so strong, so powerful.

"Let it go. Don't let your father's mistakes rule your life, Jamie," Cooper said softly, his mouth near her ear. "It's tragic that he was so broken that he killed himself, but it's not your responsibility. You can't take on a dead man's burdens. It's impossible, and it's a fight you can't win. I won't let you do this to yourself. I love you too much to let you wallow in this crap. Let it go."

"Okay, we've got five minutes," Paul Murphy said as he swung through the door.

He stopped in his tracks when he registered Cooper and the fact that Jamie was in his arms crying.

"Have we got a problem here?" he asked cautiously.

Cooper spoke up. "Something's come up. Jamie won't be fighting tonight," he said.

Murphy's eyes popped wide. "They've got a capacity crowd up there."

"Not our problem," Cooper said.

Murphy turned for the door. Jamie lifted her head from Cooper's shoulder, her stomach churning, her mind whirling.

"Wait," she said.

She felt Cooper's body stiffen beneath her hands.

"No," he said.

She looked up at him, her gaze steady. "I think I need to do this."

"No, you don't."

"I grew up in boxing gyms. I went to every fight my father ever had. There's a reason why I was drawn to this sport, why I have this fire inside me, why I'm here tonight. You once said to me that everyone who gets in the ring is fighting their own demons as well as the other guy. Maybe I need to take down my demons tonight."

Cooper closed his eyes. She could see how afraid he was for her.

"Jamie—"

"All those other fights—they were for the wrong reasons. Just once, I'd like to fight with everything I've got, with a clear mind and heart. I'd like to know why I'm out there, who I'm fighting for."

"Who? Who are you fighting for?" he asked, staring into her eyes.

"Me. This time, it's for me and no one else."

Cooper pulled her close and wrapped his arms around her, his embrace so tight it stole her breath. After a long beat, he let her go and turned to deal with her trainer.

"Get me some tape and her gloves. I'm taking over."

Murphy opened his mouth to protest, and Cooper spoke again.

"Don't worry, you'll still get your cut."

Jamie felt a surge of gratitude and relief as his words sank in. Cooper understood. This amazing man had flown all the way to Vegas to save her from herself. And even though she knew it was going to kill him to watch her slug it out in the ring against an opponent who was vastly more experienced, he was going to do it because he understood that she needed to do this.

"I love you. I'm sorry for being such a pain in the ass. Thank you for putting up with me," she said humbly.

"You can make it up to me over the next fifty odd years," he said. He checked the tape on her hands before sliding her gloves on. "I've been keeping a list."

She smirked. "I bet you have."

"It's long, too. So I'm going to have to ask you to be careful out in that ring tonight because I plan on collecting on my debts."

Jamie watched his face as he concentrated on lacing her gloves and taping the laces down. He was a man in a million. Despite all the obstacles she'd put in his way, he'd fought his way through to her.

Cooper tested her gloves, then checked her boot laces. Reaching for the Vaseline, he greased up her face as he started to talk.

"She's a southpaw, so you need to keep an eye out for her left hook. That's her knockout punch and she'll try to nail you with it early on. She's never seen you fight, so you have the advantage. You're a mystery to her, and she's going to come out cocky because you've only got three fights to your name."

"She's fast. Some of the best footwork I've ever seen," Jamie said.

Adrenaline was surging through her, her limbs tingling with it.

"You're fast, too. But you're going to have to be smarter than her. You're going to have to reel her in."

For the next few minutes, Cooper outlined his strategy. Jamie nodded, asked a couple of questions. Then Murphy checked the time and moved to the door.

"We need to go. They're about to announce you," he said.

"I'm ready," Jamie said, looking to Cooper.

"One moment."

Cooper crossed the room and scooped her father's robe off the floor. Jamie swallowed a lump as he settled it over her shoulders, the blue satin rippling in the fluorescent light.

"Now you're ready," he said.

The corridor was dim as they made their way to the auditorium. She could hear the roar of the crowd, muffled through layers of concrete, the sound getting louder and louder as they neared the exit. Needing the reassurance, she glanced back over her shoulder, just to confirm that Cooper was really there. He met her gaze steadily, as he always had. As he always would.

The glare and noise in the arena was overwhelming—flashes popping, spotlights zeroing in on her, the crowd screaming her name. Her heart pounding, Jamie made the long walk to the ring.

She was afraid of this fight, more afraid than she'd ever been before. But she also wanted to win more than ever before, too.

Cooper bounded up the steps to part the ropes for her. She slid between them and into the ring. Her father's robe billowed behind her as she lifted her hands in the air and did a single slow lap, letting the excitement in the auditorium buzz into her bloodstream.

When she was a little girl, she'd lived for fight nights. This sport was in her blood. She was a fighter, from a family of fighters.

Returning to her corner, she looked down and saw Cooper conferring with her grandfather. Her grandfather looked distressed, and she deliberately caught his eye and smiled a big, buzzy, cocky, I'm-gonna-win-this-fight smile. He stopped mid-sentence, his expression arrested. Then he slowly shut his mouth and nodded. Just the once, but she knew that her grandfather had received her unspoken message. This was going to happen. She knew what she was doing, and she wanted it for all the right reasons.

The loudspeaker came on and her opponent was announced. Cooper climbed the steps to check on her one last time and take her robe. She watched his face closely the whole time, loving him, drawing energy and power from his presence.

"I love you," she said as he prepared to descend the steps.

"I love you, too. Now go kick some ass," he said, his voice deep with emotion.

She grinned around her mouthguard and punched her gloved fists together.

"Deal."

Turning, she rolled her shoulders and bounced from foot to foot and eyed up her opponent.

She was ready.

COOPER'S PALMS were sweating. Hell, his whole body was sweating. Jamie was in the ring, and once again he was going to have to stand by and watch her get hurt.

She'd made her choice. He understood it, in his gut, if not in his head. But it was still going to be hard.

Arthur Sawyer made a clicking sound with his teeth. Cooper shot the old man a look. Arthur had been upset, to say the least, when Cooper had explained the outcome of his confrontation with Jamie. Then he'd seen her determination and clarity firsthand. She was unstoppable. Always had been, always would be.

Lucky Cooper liked his women strong and feisty.

Jamie was standing in the center of the ring with her opponent, listening to the referee. She and Roma Williams tapped gloves and retreated to their corners. Cooper's heart kicked against his ribs as the bell rang.

The fight was on.

Typical Jamie, she moved in fast and took the fight up to Williams. Six foot, black and solid, Roma Williams was tough and she took Jamie's jabs in her stride, dancing around, getting Jamie's measure. Jamie took the opportunity to land a few more punches. Cooper glanced across to see the judges marking their sheets.

Good. Jamie had clocked up some early points, just as they'd discussed.

Williams didn't take long to join the party. Having watched Jamie move, she began to turn up the heat, peppering Jamie with jabs and crosses, keeping Jamie busy blocking and ducking and weaving. Jamie took hits, her head bobbing on her neck, sweat flying off her face as leather struck flesh.

Midway through the first round, Arthur leaned across and seized Cooper's arm in alarm.

"What's she doing? She's thinking with her feet again!" the old man hissed, his eyes wide.

Jamie had reverted to old habits, her feet lifting and then dropping as she quelled the instinct to kick her opponent, each aborted move making her vulnerable to attack.

"Must be the pressure," Arthur said, his face screwed up with concern.

Cooper narrowed his gaze and watched the opposite corner where Williams's trainer stood with his arms crossed, eyes intent on the action. Had he noticed Jamie's weakness? Would he direct Roma to zero in on those fatal hesitations of Jamie's in the next round?

The women continued to exchange blows, dancing forward, engaging, falling back, circling, always circling. After what seemed like forever, the bell rang and they both retreated to their corners.

Cooper slid the stool through the ropes and slipped through after it. He held his hand out for Jamie's mouthguard. She spat it onto his hand and he rinsed it over the bucket while she washed her mouth out.

"Do you think they bought it?" she asked in between trying to catch her breath.

"He noticed. We'll have to see what she plans to do about it. If she tries to take advantage, you know what you've got to do," he said.

She nodded, dropping her head back against the ropes. He looked at her long, strong, lean body, her beautiful face, her startling silver eyes.

He loved her more than he'd ever thought it was possible to love another human being. He wanted her to win this very badly.

"You can do this, Spitfire," he said.

Her mouth tugged up into a half smile. Aware of the clock counting down, he offered her the mouthguard, checked her cheeks and brow, and mopped the sweat off her chest.

Then he was back through the ropes, the stool following him. He'd barely turned to face the ring before the second round bell was reverberating around the arena.

Williams came out more strongly this time, keen to score points. Jamie maintained her awkward footwork, offering the other woman openings to exploit. Cooper watched in frustration as the other woman refused to bite. Instead, Williams concentrated on her own fight plan, wearing Jamie down with an unrelenting barrage of body blows.

Head blows might knock a fighter out, but the body was a much larger target and therefore harder to protect. There was no way Jamie could stop all the blows Williams rained down her. By the end of the second round, she was hurting. He saw it in her eyes as she dropped onto the stool. He pressed the No-Swell against her brow and cheekbones, and offered her what he could.

"She's trying to wind you. Keep an eye out for her right uppercut—she always jabs with her left before she goes for your solar plexus."

Jamie stared at him, her silver eyes desperate as she sucked in air.

"Do I stop trying to bait her?" she asked, gasping for breath. "Come out hard, do what I can with everything I've got?"

"No. She'll bite. I know she will," he said.

Jamie nodded her acceptance of his advice. He slid back to the safe side of the ropes as the bell rang.

He suffered through another round of watching Jamie get pounded as she offered up openings again and again to her opponent. As the bell rang at the end of the third round, he had to stop himself from sweeping Jamie into his arms and refusing to let her go.

She would hate him for not letting her fight her own battles. She would always want to prove herself first, before she looked to anyone else for help. It was a fundamental part of who she was.

They didn't discuss strategy this time as she sank onto the stool. Jamie gulped air, rinsed her mouth out and simply watched him, her gaze absolutely trusting.

He hoped like hell he'd done something to earn that trust. That he hadn't offered her bad advice and held her back for no reason.

"It'll be this round," he predicted. "Stay alert."

His heart surged into his throat when a minute into the fourth round, Williams at last took the bait. Jamie offered up a hesitation, the merest faltering of her footwork, and Williams stepped in and tried to lay Jamie out with her left hook. The punch flew through the air, unstoppable, apparently impossible to survive. Jamie rolled with it, stumbling back a step. Her blood up, Williams moved after her, ready to finish Jamie off.

Which was when Jamie stepped around the other woman, using Williams's own momentum against her, and slammed a right hook into the angle of the other woman's jaw.

The world seemed to stop as Williams swayed on her feet. The crowd roared. Cooper held his breath. Jamie popped a straight-armed jab high on the other woman's cheekbone, sealing the deal. Williams went down like a felled tree, her body slapping against the canvas.

There was no need for a count. She was out cold.

Relief surging through him, Cooper rushed the ropes as Jamie was declared the winner. She punched the air, throwing her head back. He reached her, wrapping her in her father's robe. She spat her mouthguard to one side and kissed him, her face streaming with tears.

"I did it," she said. "I did it."

"I know, baby, I know," he said, pressing a kiss into her neck and holding her close.

Thank God she was safe.

The crowd stood for Jamie and cheered as she walked away from the ring. Near the exit, a camera crew waited. This time Jamie didn't turn her back on them.

She stepped up and stared down the barrel of the camera, her beautiful face very serious. Ignoring the journalist's questions, she spoke into the microphone.

"I want to dedicate tonight's fight to my father, Jack Sawyer. He was a great man, a great fighter, and I loved him very much," she said.

Her piece said, she turned away, leaving the journalist gasping like a landed fish.

Cooper was still laughing when they entered the change room.

"Someone's going to get a reputation for being difficult with the press if she keeps that up," he said, "as well as a reputation as a knockout artist."

She shot him a wary look and he cocked his head at her. "What?"

"I was thinking that maybe you'd be ready for me to retire after tonight," she said carefully.

He studied her, her face shiny with Vaseline and sweat, her color high, her hair wet with perspiration.

"You can't give this up. Not yet. It's part of you, for whatever reason. You're a warrior woman," he said.

Her mouth opened and she blinked at him. "You always *know*," she said, her voice low with emotion. "How do you always know what's in my heart?"

"Because we're the same, baby," he said, drawing her close. "We're two halves of a whole."

He kissed her lips, her eyelids, the curve of her neck.

"What about you? What about having to watch me fight?" she asked, breaking the kiss to eye him worriedly. "If you can't stand it, I'll walk away. I swear it."

He pushed the hair off her forehead and traced the curve of her ear with his fingers.

"I'm tough. Before this training gig, I did a little time in the ring myself, you know. I know what it's like to want to own that space. And you're a beautiful fighter, Jamie. There's no way I would take that away from you. As long as you're out there for the right reasons, I'll stand beside you."

"I love you," she said, gripping his face in her taped hands.

"I feel the same way," he said. They both broke into big, slow grins.

"You're going to have to do better than that," she said.

"Yeah?"

"A whole lot better," she said, reaching for the stud on his jeans.

He threw a glance over his shoulder toward the door. "Your grandfather will be here any minute," he said.

"No, he won't. He's a smart man. He knows what happens when I win," she said, popping the buttons on his fly.

He shuddered as she found his cock and wrapped her fingers around it.

"What happens when you win?" he asked, reaching for the lower edge of her sports crop.

"I get horny. Really, really horny," she breathed.

"Huh. I knew there was a reason I loved this sport."

* * * * *

Look for Sarah Mayberry's next Harlequin Blaze novel!
Coming October 2008

The editors at Harlequin Blaze have never been afraid to push the limits—tempting readers with the forbidden, whetting their appetites with a wide variety of story lines. But now we're breaking the final barrier—the time barrier.

In July, watch for BOUND TO PLEASE by fan favorite Hope Tarr, Harlequin Blaze's first ever historical romance—a story that's truly Blaze-worthy in every sense.

Here's a sneak peek...

Brianna stretched out beside Ewan, languid as a cat, and promptly fell asleep. Midday sunshine streamed into the chamber, bathing her lovely, long-limbed body in golden light, the sea-scented breeze wafting inside to dry the damp red-gold tendrils curling about her flushed face. Propping himself up on one elbow, Ewan slid his gaze over her. She looked beautiful and whole, satisfied and sated, and altogether happier than he had so far seen her. A slight smile curved her beautiful lips as though she must be in the midst of a lovely dream. She'd molded her lush, lovely body to his and laid her head in the curve of his shoulder and settled in to sleep beside him. For the longest while he lay there turned toward her, content to watch her sleep, at near perfect peace.

Not wholly perfect, for she had yet to answer his marriage proposal. Still, she wanted to make a baby with him, and Ewan no longer viewed her plan as the travesty he once had. He wanted children—sons to carry on after him, though a bonny little daughter with flame-colored hair would be nice, too. But he also wanted more than to simply plant his seed and be on his way. He wanted to lie beside Brianna night upon night as she increased, rub soothing unguents into the swell of her belly, knead the ache from her back and make slow, gentle love to her. He wanted to hold his newly born child in his arms and look down into Brianna's tired but radiant face and blot the perspiration from her brow and be a husband to her in every way.

He gave her a gentle nudge. "Brie?"

"Hmmm?"

She rolled onto her side and he captured her against his chest. One arm wrapped about her waist, he bent to her ear and asked, "Do you think we might have just made a baby?"

Her eyes remained closed, but he felt her tense against him. "I don't know. We'll have to wait and see."

He stroked his hand over the flat plane of her belly. "You're so small and tight it's hard to imagine you increasing."

"All women increase no matter how large or small they start out. I may not grow big as a croft, but I'll be big enough, though I have hopes I may not waddle like a duck, at least not too badly."

The reference to his fair-day teasing was not lost on him. He grinned. "Brianna MacLeod grown so large she must sit still for once in her life. I'll need the proof of my own eyes to believe it."

Despite their banter, he felt his spirits dip. Assuming they were so blessed, he wouldn't have the chance to see her thus. By then he would be long gone, restored to his clan according to the sad bargain they'd struck. He opened his mouth to ask her to marry him again and then clamped it closed, not wanting to spoil the moment, but the unspoken words weighed like a millstone on his heart.

The damnable bargain they'd struck was proving to be a devil's pact indeed.

* * * * *

Will these two star-crossed lovers
find their sexily-ever-after?
Find out in BOUND TO PLEASE
by Hope Tarr, available in July
wherever Harlequin® Blaze™ books are sold.

Harlequin Blaze marks new territory with its first historical novel!

For years readers have trusted the Harlequin Blaze series to entertain them with a variety of stories— Now Blaze is breaking down the final barrier— the time barrier!

Welcome to Blaze Historicals—all the sexiness you love in a Blaze novel, all the adventure of a historical romance. It's the best of both worlds!

Don't miss the first book in this exciting new miniseries:

BOUND TO PLEASE
by Hope Tarr

New laird Brianna MacLeod knows she can't protect her land or her people without a man by her side. So what else can she do—she kidnaps one! Only, she doesn't expect to find herself the one enslaved....

Available in July
wherever Harlequin books are sold.

www.eHarlequin.com

HB79411

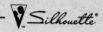

SPECIAL EDITION™

NEW YORK TIMES BESTSELLING AUTHOR

DIANA PALMER

A brand-new Long, Tall Texans novel

HEART OF STONE

Feeling unwanted and unloved, Keely returns
to Jacobsville and to Boone Sinclair, a rancher
troubled by his own past. Boone has always
seemed reserved, but now Keely discovers a
sensuality with him that quickly turns to love. Can
they each see past their own scars to let love in?

*Available September 2008
wherever you buy books.*

Visit Silhouette Books at www.eHarlequin.com   SSE24921

Silhouette®

Romantic
SUSPENSE

Sparked by Danger, Fueled by Passion.

Conard County: The Next Generation

When he learns the truth about his father, military
man Ethan Parish is determined to reunite with his
long-lost family in Wyoming. On his way into town,
he clashes with policewoman Connie Halloran,
whose captivating beauty entices him. When
Connie's daughter is threatened, Ethan must use
his military skills to keep her safe. Together they
race against time to find the little girl and confront
the dangers inherent in family secrets.

Look for

A Soldier's Homecoming

by *New York Times*
bestselling author
Rachel Lee

Available in July wherever you buy books.

Visit Silhouette Books at www.eHarlequin.com   SRS27589

REQUEST YOUR FREE BOOKS!

2 FREE NOVELS
PLUS 2
FREE GIFTS!

HARLEQUIN®

Blaze™

Red-hot reads!

YES! Please send me 2 FREE Harlequin® Blaze™ novels and my 2 FREE gifts (gifts are worth about $10). After receiving them, if I don't wish to receive any more books, I can return the shipping statement marked "cancel". If I don't cancel, I will receive 6 brand-new novels every month and be billed just $4.24 per book in the U.S. or $4.71 per book in Canada, plus 25¢ shipping and handling per book and applicable taxes, if any*. That's a savings of 15% or more off the cover price! I understand that accepting the 2 free books and gifts places me under no obligation to buy anything. I can always return a shipment and cancel at any time. Even if I never buy another book, the two free books and gifts are mine to keep forever.

151 HDN ERVA   351 HDN ERUX

Name	(PLEASE PRINT)	
Address		Apt. #
City	State/Prov.	Zip/Postal Code

Signature (if under 18, a parent or guardian must sign)

Mail to the **Harlequin Reader Service:**
IN U.S.A.: P.O. Box 1867, Buffalo, NY 14240-1867
IN CANADA: P.O. Box 609, Fort Erie, Ontario L2A 5X3

Not valid to current subscribers of Harlequin Blaze books.

Want to try two free books from another line?
Call 1-800-873-8635 or visit www.morefreebooks.com.

* Terms and prices subject to change without notice. N.Y. residents add applicable sales tax. Canadian residents will be charged applicable provincial taxes and GST. Offer not valid in Quebec. This offer is limited to one order per household. All orders subject to approval. Credit or debit balances in a customer's account(s) may be offset by any other outstanding balance owed by or to the customer. Please allow 4 to 6 weeks for delivery. Offer available while quantities last.

Your Privacy: Harlequin Books is committed to protecting your privacy. Our Privacy Policy is available online at www.eHarlequin.com or upon request from the Reader Service. From time to time we make our lists of customers available to reputable third parties who may have a product or service of interest to you. If you would prefer we not share your name and address, please check here. ☐

HB08R

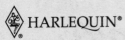

HARLEQUIN®

American ★ Romance®

MADE IN TEXAS

It's the happiest day of Hannah Callahan's life
when she brings her new daughter home to Texas.
And Joe Daugherty would make a perfect father
to complete their unconventional family. But the
world-hopping writer never stays in one place
long enough. Can Joe trust in love enough to
finally get the family he's always wanted?

LOOK FOR

Hannah's Baby

BY

CATHY GILLEN THACKER

*Available July
wherever you buy books.*

LOVE, HOME & HAPPINESS

www.eHarlequin.com   HAR75222

HARLEQUIN®
Blaze™

COMING NEXT MONTH

#405 WHAT I DID ON MY SUMMER VACATION
Thea Divine, Debbi Rawlins, Samantha Hunter
A Sizzling Summer Collection
Three single women end up with a fling worth writing about in this Blazing summer collection. Whether they spend their time in the city, in the woods or at the beach, their reports are bound to be strictly X-rated!

#406 INCOGNITO Kate Hoffmann
Forbidden Fantasies
Haven't you ever wished you could be someone else? Lily Hart has. So when she's mistaken for a promiscuous celebrity, she jumps at the chance to live out the erotic lifestyle she's always envied. After all, nobody will find out. Or will they?

#407 BOUND TO PLEASE Hope Tarr
Blaze Historicals
Blaze marks new territory with its first historical novel! New laird Brianna MacLeod knows she can't protect her land or her people without a man by her side. So, she kidnaps one! Only, she never expects to find herself the one enslaved....

#408 HEATED RUSH Leslie Kelly
The Wrong Bed: Again and Again
Annie Davis is in trouble. Her big family reunion is looming, and she needs a stand-in man—fast. Her solution? Bachelor number twenty at the charity bachelor auction. But there's more to her rent-a-date than meets the eye....

#409 BED ON ARRIVAL Kelley St. John
The Sexth Sense
Jenee Vicknair is keeping a wicked secret. Every night she has wild, mind-blowing sex with a perfect stranger. They never exchange words—their bodies say everything that needs to be said. If only her lover didn't vanish into thin air the moment the satisfaction was over....

#410 FLASHPOINT Jill Shalvis
American Heroes: The Firefighters
Zach Thomas might put out fires for a living, but when the sexy firefighter meets EMT Brooke O'Brian, all he wants to do is stoke her flames. Still, can Brooke count on him to take the heat if the sparks between them flare out of control?

www.eHarlequin.com

HBCNM0608